Devlin's Door

Forests of the Fae: Book One

A novel

by K. Kibbee

Incorgnito Publishing Press
A division of Market Management Group, LLC
300 E. Bellevue Drive, Suite 208 Pasadena, CA 91101

SECOND EDITION

Printed in the United States of America

ISBN: 978-0-9969111-1-5

10 9 8 7 6 5 4 3 2 1

Acknowledgments

I'd like to extend my deep and sincere thanks to all those who contributed to the development and actualization of this book.

To my husband, Sean: Your insightful feedback on this and the following books in the series, as well as the support and encouragement that you've offered throughout my years as an aspiring author, have been invaluable to me.

To my Mama: That extra little push you gave me that launched me into the sky and forced me to fly has made me realize my dreams. And for that, I'll be forever grateful.

To my publishers, Michael Conant and Janice Bini of Incorgnito Publishing Press: Thank you for noticing me in the fray of floundering, would-be authors, and extending a hand up. I appreciate your graciousness and your shared passion for my work.

To my illustrator, Liga Klavina: Your artistic gifts, amiable nature and kindness have impressed me ever since I wandered across one of your mesmerizing works by happenstance. Thank you for bearing all of the ups and downs of this cover art process, and for giving my book such a beautiful jacket to wear as it's introduced to the world!

Contents

Chapter One

The rain was relentless, as if determined to drown the earth. The trees outside the train window whizzed by like watercolors running down a canvas. Anne pretended to study them, hoping the little boy in the seat opposite her would notice and think it rude to interrupt. He'd been staring at her since Tacoma, his beetle eyes burrowing deeper as the minutes ticked by. His chubby freckled cheeks twitched with energy. "Whatchya lookin' at?" he asked.

"Hmmmm?" Connecting raindrops on the glass, Anne formed a horse and a one-eared Mickey Mouse that promptly merged and then washed away. Perhaps if she didn't look at him he'd pester someone else.

The boy scooted sideways until he was square in view and then he leaned forward on his bench. "Whatchya lookin' at?" he repeated.

"Nothing, I guess. Just trees." All hope was lost. Anne surrendered her full attention, although she felt he'd stolen it. The boy was wearing a crisp, blue button-up dress shirt, along with khakis,and a ball cap. Fixed on the lapel of his shirt was a shiny pin in the shape of a caboose that read "VIP RIDER." Anne recognized the pin from the brochure—an identifier for young riders who required supervision from employee chaperones.

"I'm Jeremy," he told her. "I've seen all that stuff, like, a million times. I've probably rode this train more times than anybody."

"Oh yeah?" Anne resumed her study of the muddied landscape.

"Yeah. I'm a V-I-P."

Anne rolled her eyes at her reflection in the window. "Wow, cool."

Jeremy puffed out his chest and then craned forward, elbows perched on his knees. Hovering around five feet, he was a few inches shorter than Anne. But, bent down as he was, it seemed more like a foot.

"Yeah, I'm headed to Portland today. My dad lives there. I go back and forth a lot between him and my mom's house in Seattle." Jeremy leaned in a little closer. The smell of Fritos drifted from his breath as he asked, "So, where're you headed?"

"Woodland," she replied, suppressing a groan.

"Oh, yeah? I've been there." Sensing encouragement, Jeremy inched forward. His breath was close and hot. *Were those Chili-Cheese Fritos?* "Pretty small town. Why you goin' there?"

He suddenly felt too close. "My parents are sending me down there for the summer," Anne explained just as a middle-aged woman in a blue blazer appeared at her side.

"You two kiddos doing alright?" the woman asked. She was wearing a caboose pin similar to Jeremy's and as she narrowed her eyes at him, Anne noted a familiarity between the two. "This one isn't givin' you too much trouble, is he?"

Anne glanced at Jeremy, who'd resumed his original spot on the bench and was wearing a very innocent-looking grin. "Oh no, everything's fine," she replied.

"Well, alrighty then. You need anything, you give me a holler." As the attendant waddled out of sight, Anne silently rejoiced that at thirteen she was just above the "VIP Rider" threshold that would've saddled her with a permanent babysitter.

"Thanks." Jeremy settled in his seat, somehow more human. "So, why'd your folks send you to a cruddy place like Woodland for the summer?"

Anne had been asking the same question for weeks, and Jeremy suddenly became infinitely more interesting to her. "I dunno. Cruel and unusual punishment for getting a C in Biology two semesters running?"

Jeremy chuckled. His little beetle eyes sparkled as his belly jiggled.

Anne sighed, relenting. "I guess they just didn't have any other options." She glanced outside again, thinking about the clouds that were probably passing by her mother's airplane window. "They're both doctors and they got a kinda neat missionary job together, doing medical aid in Uganda this summer."

Jeremy's beetles swelled. "Whoa, cool! Would'a been awesome

to go!"

"Yeah, you're tellin' me. But instead I get stuck with my aunt 'n uncle and witch of a cousin in po-dunk Woodland."

Another empty smile wrapped in a royal blue blazer appeared in the aisle alongside them, just as Anne felt her mood souring. "Can I tempt you two with any snacks?" asked a tall, square-faced man with one lazy eye. He dangled a packet of peanuts in front of Jeremy, and then fanned his free hand towards a metal cart he'd been pushing. "Got soda pop, here. And pretzels, too, if you like." Anne was too busy deciding which of his eyes to focus on to even look at the snacks.

"I'll have my usual, Monroe," Jeremy declared, resuming his insufferable disposition.

Monroe emptied a half-can of 7UP into a plastic cup and then handed it to Jeremy, along with a shiny sack of almonds. "And for the lady?"

"Oh, no — no thanks. None for me."

Monroe nodded, his good eye fixed on Anne as she struggled to hold it. "Very well." The wonky rear wheel on his cart squeaked like a mouse as he rolled it out of sight.

On the heels of Monroe's departure, a succession of beeps erupted overhead, drawing attention to the speakers mounted above the car's luggage racks. Watching them expectantly, Anne was certain they swelled like inflating balloons. "ATTENTION AMTRAK

RIDERS, WE ARE APPROACHING THE KELSO WASHING-
TON STATION. FOR THOSE OF YOU EXITING, PLEASE PRE-
PARE YOUR BELONGINGS."

"I've been to Kelso," Jeremy announced, chewing an almond.
"Nothin' special if you ask me."

Anne only nodded, once again wishing he hadn't sat across from
her. She could feel the train slowing. People were pulling bags from
the bins, zipping up cases and generally buzzing about. They began
to line up in the aisle like early shoppers for a Black Friday sale.
As the line leaked back to Anne and Jeremy's section of the train, a
round Hispanic woman and her two young boys came to stand beside
them. The younger of the boys was goading his brother, pinching
him every time he faced forward. When the eldest had finally had his
fill, and pinched back, the younger one wailed like a banshee. Their
mother smacked them both. Soon, the train came to a full stop and
the line began to move toward the exits. Anne watched as the older
boy sped up and darted in front of his mother. She momentarily felt
jealous that he could escape his tormenter while she could not.

When the train lurched into motion again, Jeremy downed the
remainder of his nuts and drained his cup. "So Woodland, huh?
That's just about as nowhere as you get."

Anne nodded. "Yup."

"Well, that is, unless you count the Nowhere Town."

Anne had been watching black-and-white blobs in the distance grow larger and form cows, but she shifted her attention in a flash. "Waddaya mean, 'Nowhere Town?'"

Jeremy smiled wide, his lips curling until the grin turned devilish. He had almond gunk stuck between his two front teeth. "Ah-ha, you don't know about it," he jeered, sliding across his bench seat and once again positioning himself far too close for Anne's taste. "I guess it doesn't surprise me. But I know about most everything along the route. Guess I forget that not everyone has been lotsa places, like me."

Anne rolled her eyes. "Yeah, okay."

Jeremy shifted back a bit and tipped his stubby nose in the air. He was eerily quiet.

"So, you gonna tell me?" Anne asked far too eagerly.

The shrill beeping that had shaken the overhead speakers at the previous stop again what seemed like only moments ago cascaded through the car again, giving Anne a start. "ATTENTION, RIDERS. PLEASE NOTE THAT WE ARE APPROACHING KALAMA, WASHINGTON. OUR NEXT STOP OF WOODLAND, WASHINGTON, WILL FOLLOW IN APPROXIMATELY TEN MINUTES."

Anne remained fixed on Jeremy, who still sat smugly silent across from her. "C'mon. I've gotta get off soon," she pleaded.

Jeremy inched forward. "Well, okay," he began, wagging his head, "But you owe me."

"Uh-huh." Anne bit her lip and scooted towards him.

The rain had stopped, and as the clouds parted, a bright orange sun burst from its hiding place. The rays shined in through the railcar's window and lit Jeremy's eyes as he spoke. "We should be coming to it soon," he told her. "You'll see the peaks of the houses, way back there in the forest." He pointed at a hill in the distance, where Anne saw only unending green. "No one lives there. The houses are all falling apart, and the forest has grown right into 'em."

Anne stared hard at the flock of trees that Jeremy had called her attention to, willing a sliver of rooftop to appear. He studied her, still smiling, and continued. "People used to live there, of course…back in the old days. Used to be a really nice place, with all those big, fancy houses." He joined her line of sight, as the train came closer to the hillside. "But then one day they just all up and vanished."

"Vanished?" Anne could not tear her eyes from the green.

"Yup, vanished."

Beep, beep, beeeeeeeeeeeeeeeeep! "ATTENTION, AMTRAK PASSENGERS WITH A WOODLAND, WASHINGTON, DESTINATION. YOUR STATION IS APPROACHING. PLEASE PREPARE BY GATHERING YOUR BELONGINGS."

"Hey, isn't that you?" Jeremy asked.

"What? Who?" Anne was still staring at the nearing hillside. She imagined dozens of peaks emerging from the trees, like iceberg caps with empty bellies hidden beneath the waves of green. "Did you say something?"

When she finally turned to look at him, Anne found Jeremy had risen and was unlatching the wide ivory bin mounted over their seats. "Your stop. It's coming up," he said.

"Oh! Crap!" Anne joined him, fishing her lavender backpack and an old tweed suitcase from the rack, before he lofted his own bags back in. The suitcase belonged to her father, and she felt a pang of sadness rip through her as she gripped its handle. She'd never been separated from her parents for longer than a day or two. Three months without them would be unbearable.

Jeremy latched the overhead compartment closed and resumed his place by the window. As Anne gathered her things and pondered a proper farewell, he began gyrating in his seat like popping corn. "There! Right there!" he called, pointing wildly out the window. "I can see one of them!"

Anne abandoned her bags and rushed to his side. "Really? Where?" She gawked at the vast forest as if expecting a fireworks display to begin. "I don't see it. Am I looking where I'm supposed to?"

"Haha, gotchya!" Jeremy was clutching his quaking belly, his pointer finger now aimed squarely at her. "Oh ,man, you should'a seen your face. I totally got you!"

Her face twisted in a knot as Anne steadied herself against the seat opposite his and the train lurched to a stop. "Goodbye, Jeremy," she said with a short, little snarl, returning to her luggage. She marched down the aisle, and out of his sight, but she could still hear him laughing.

A large wooden sign at the head of the terminal read, "Welcome to Woodland," but as Anne stepped off the train and met the three sour faces of her relatives, she felt anything but welcome.

Anne's uncle, Pat, was dressed head to toe in camo, and a foot-long beard covered the better part of his chest. It fell in a furry pool onto his beer belly, where it parted like the Red Sea. "Get on over here, girl, and gimme those bags," he called.

Anne forced a smile and made up the distance between them at a slow pace. Her aunt, Claudia, studied her approach with a notice-able sneer. "Just look at you," she greeted, bugging her blue-shad-owed eyes. "All growed up and travelin' across the country in style."

"I don't know that I'd call it style," Anne admitted, handing her bags off to Pat. "Or cross country." Her aunt embraced her in an awkward hug that smelled of cigarette smoke.

"Well, go on," Claudia encouraged, already releasing her niece. "Hug your cousin."

Anne's cousin Lexie was standing behind her father, attention fixed on the iPhone in her palm. It had a neon pink case with rub-ber rabbit ears, and as she tapped it over and over again with her thumb, its little ears quaked. "Hey, Lexie," Anne greeted her, walk-ing towards her with all the enthusiasm of a death row inmate on the Green Mile.

Lexie lifted her head as if it were very heavy. Her eyes stayed glued to the phone. "Oh, yeah. Hey."

"Dammit, Lexie! Put down the damn phone and hug your cousin!" Anne could feel warm breath tickling the back of her neck when Claudia spoke, as though a fuming bull was looming just over her shoulder. Somehow that contempt infected Lexie, who seemed a willing host. She screwed her mouth into a snarl and stalked towards Anne, squeezing her without as much as a word. As they parted, her pale blue eyes lingered and she smiled far too sweetly.

It was a short walk to the car but Anne kept a distance from her relatives such as she would have from strangers. Her uncle's SUV smelled of chewing tobacco and the floorboards were caked with dried mud. Trapped in the backseat with her cousin, Anne directed her full attention outside, studying the downtown storefronts as they passed. Though they lived "in the sticks" (or so her uncle said), the town of Woodland was small, and they'd reached the tan rambler in under ten minutes. The house was dim and unkempt. It felt neglected, as if its hearth and heart had gone cold for lack of tending.

"You'll be bunkin' with Lex," Pat explained, pointing towards a door at the end of the entry hall where a "NO TRESPASSING" sign hung beside a pink and purple plaque that read "Lexie's Room."

"Great," Lexie moaned as she passed them and continued down the hall. Anne followed with heavy footsteps, cursing her parents all the way. Nearing Lexie's room she spied a gruesome skull leering at her from the "O" in the "NO TRESPASSING" mandate. It had a veiny eyeball popping from its left socket and a snake twisting from its right. Anne stepped past it with a degree of caution, but as she made a move to cross the threshold, Lexie's arm blocked her path. "Okay, kid," Lexie began, "If you're gonna stay in my room, there's gonna be rules. You see all this stuff?" Lexie fanned her hand wide past heaps of clothes, a teetering tower of CDs, peeling posters and an unmade bed. "All this stuff is MINE. And that means you keep your snotty little paws off it. No looky, no touchy. Got it?"

Anne nodded.

Lexie had one hand on her hip and she wagged her head as she went on. "And while we're at it, let's add no talkie to that list. It's not my fault your stupid parents dumped you here, and I'm not gonna babysit you and have you ruining my summer."

"I'm not a baby, ya know." Anne's face flushed. "You're what, two years older than me?"

Once, on an episode of "Wild Kingdom," Anne had seen a lioness watch as a hyena stole the dinner it had taken her a full hour to catch. The same eyes that had burrowed through that weak little hyena stared back at her now. "It'll be three, next month," Lexie growled. "Assuming I let you live that long."

Claudia appeared behind Anne just as she was bracing for an attack. "Well, you don't look like you've done much settling in. Guess you'll have to do it after dinner. Pizza is nuked and on the table."

17

Pizza had never sounded quite so inviting. Anne trailed close behind her aunt without a second look at Lexie.

Gathered around the oak dining table, Anne examined the shriveled olives on her pizza and wondered how old they were. "So, what kinda mischief you lookin' to get up to this summer?" her uncle asked just as she'd begun scraping them off.

"Errr, ummm…I dunno."

"Well, there's all sorts around here." Pat's eyes twinkled as Anne met them. "Good fishin' down on the river, and there's a swimming hole not a stone's throw from our back pasture."

"Oh Patty, girls don't care nothin' about that," Claudia interjected. Her open mouth was bursting and Anne recoiled as a pepperoni slice shined through her teeth like an eclipsed moon. "She'd probably rather head out shoppin' with Lexie and her crowd."

Lexie was sneering as Anne chanced a look at her. "Oh, no, that's okay. I'm not a big shopper," Anne stumbled behind a forced smile.

"See Claude, she's the outdoorsy type!" Tiny flecks of Parmesan cheese peppered Pat's beard and fell like snow as he spoke.

Anne imagined herself drowning in camouflage and hunkered beside him in a hunter's blind. "Well, maybe not that outdoorsy," she piped.

Claudia had swallowed her mouthful, but as she spoke an olive chunk wedged between her two front teeth. "So you're not gonna shop and you're not gonna fish. What are you gonna get up to? Can't have you sulking around the house all summer!"

Anne wracked her brain. "Well, umm…there was this kid on the train and he was telling me about a town close to here that sounded pretty neat. I might like to check that out. That is, if it exists. I'm not really sure if he was pulling my leg or not. He was kind of a jerk."

Pat drained his Budweiser bottle and leveled his eyes at Anne. "And what town was that?"

"You talkin' about Kalama?" Claudia asked, her lined eyebrows arching into perfect crescents.

"I'm not really sure," Anne confessed. "He never said a name. I think maybe he called it Nowhere Town."

Pat set his bottle down with a thud. "Oh no, that's no place you'd wanna visit. That's no place for a young girl, or anyone with half a mind, for that matter."

"Damn straight." Claudia had freed the olive and now fixed all of her attentions squarely upon Anne. "I don't want you goin' around that town at all this summer. You got me?"

Anne dumbly nodded, her mind contesting her head.

"Oh, jeez. What's the big deal?" Lexie was staring at her lap. The light from her cell phone screen shone upwards, casting her like a jack-o-lantern. "Ooooh, boo…the big, scary Nowhere Town. Everybody hide! It's gonna getchya!" She snickered, never raising her head.

Across the table, Pat was tearing another slice of pizza from the pie. "The town ain't whatchya got to worry about. It's all the bums and felons that camp out there. They've been squattin' in those old, abandoned houses for years now. Place is a filthy, dangerous mess and chock fulla fellas that mean nothin' but harm to some dumb girl wanderin' around out there." He took a massive bite and glanced at his empty beer bottle with a look of longing.

"And I ain't gonna be the one to call your folks and tell 'em to come pick you up in pieces!" Claudia announced, snatching the last piece of pepperoni from the greasy cardboard Dominos box just as Pat was eyeing it.

"Oh, my God, you guys are so friggin' paranoid!" Lexie exclaimed. Finally interested enough to give the conversation her full attention, she set her darkened phone on the table and took a swig of diet cola. "You make it sound like the boogeyman lives out there or something!" She rolled her eyes and looked straight at Anne. "They're just tryin' to scare you."

"We're trying to keep her from getting chopped up into teeny bits!" Claudia grumbled.

"What-ev." Lexie shot back, briefly locking eyes with Anne. "I think it's kinda cool that she's into that stuff." For a moment, it seemed a connection was made, though Lexie soon scooped up her phone and redirected her attention there. Anne's gaze lingered, perhaps hungry for a long-relished taste of something she'd only had teasers of over the years. She studied Lexie's honey-blonde high-lights and porcelain skin, the way that her pretty, pink lips pouted as she passed over words on the screen. It wasn't until later on that evening in her bedroom that Lexie revealed she'd been reading a text from her friend Brittany, who had decided to head to her father's house in New York for the summer.

"I'm totally bummed," she whimpered, drawing a pink-and-white polka-dot pajama top over her head. "We were supposed to hang out this summer."

Anne looked out the open door, down the hallway into the bath-room and wondered if Lexie would think her prudish if she ducked out to change in private. "Yeah, that sucks." When Anne turned back to feign a potty break, Lexie had her phone in hand yet again.

"Oh, cool!" Lexie's eyes lit as she looked up. "We're all gonna hang out tomorrow. Big send-off before Brittany leaves."

Anne smiled, glancing at her PJs. "Neat." She snagged them and turned to make her way towards the bathroom.

"Hey, you wanna come with us?"

Play it cool, Anne. Play it cool. "Yeah, sure." Anne spun around and eagerly returned to Lexie's bedside as if she were taking a seat at the popular kids' lunch table. Squeezing her eyes tightly closed, she shed her t-shirt and replaced it with the pajama top.

"Cool." Lexie plugged her phone into its charger and collapsed onto the bed. "Best part is, we're headed to Nowhere Town."

Chapter Two

A Longshoreman, Pat headed out to work early and Claudia slept well into late morning. This provided Lexie and Anne a wide berth in which to flit away to Nowhere Town undetected. Lexie lent Anne the better of her two bikes, and by nine a.m. they were dressed, fed and speeding down a deserted country road towards adventure. The cool morning wind whipped at Anne's long hair, and she released her handlebars and sailed down a steep grade of the road, as if flying.

"It's just up ahead," Lexie promised, crossing in front of her cousin and hugging the emerald evergreens that lined the street. A dirt cutout appeared not fifty feet ahead, and Anne leaned her weight into the bike and bore right as Lexie did. This new road was dusty and full of ruts. Anne bounced to and fro as the bike seat hammered her nether regions. Up ahead, Lexie was seamlessly dodging all the road hazards like a dancer performing an intricate ballet.

The forest sprung up before them like a misplaced wonder. There, beyond all the brown and barren fields, was a wall of green. Anne was enchanted in an instant.

Lexie slowed her bike, and leapt off mid-pedal, before abandoning it in the brush. "Here, check it out," she called to Anne, motioning towards a line of rocks just at the forest's border. "It's the ring."

Anne dismounted her bike and wheeled it over. Stopping beside her cousin, she followed Lexie's outstretched fingertip to a series of shiny, black boulders embedded in the ground. They formed a curved line extending in both directions that continued into the deep, green underbrush. "What is it?"

"I just said, dummy. It's the ring."

Anne traced the line of round little rocks with her eyes. "Umm, okay. What's the ring?"

"Oh, my God, you're such a townie," Lexie scoffed. "It's the ring that goes all the way around the town. It's supposed to be magic, or sacred, or something like that." She nudged one of the perfectly round rocks with the toe of her sneaker. "See for yourself. You can't move those rocks for nothin'."

Anne approached the ring, noting that not only was each of the rocks identical to its neighbor but that each was also touching the other, if only just. She bent down to inspect the stone that Lexie had nudged, keeping a wary distance. Deep, inky black, the stone was so glossy that it reflected Anne's face back as clearly as a mirror. Lexie kicked at her heel. "Waddaya, afraid it's gonna bite you?"

"No!" Shielding her slow-moving hand from Lexie's eyes, Anne reached out and touched the stone. It was cool, almost icy. She traced her pointer finger along it until she ran into the adjoining boulder and then gave it her full grip. "It must be stuck," she decided, bearing her weight against the rock. "Or maybe set in concrete?"

"Nope," Lexie returned, head high. "It's magic." She lifted her bike gingerly over the rocks, climbed back on and lit off down the trail on the opposite side.

Groaning, Anne followed suit and called "Wait up!" as Lexie's golden locks vanished into the brush. The forest path was smoother but narrow, with blankets of oversized clovers encroaching on either side. Anne marveled at the towering timber as she whizzed past it, trying to catch up.

A flash of blonde beaconed ahead as Lexie slowed her bike. "Hurry up! Everybody else is probably already there!"

Anne stood on her pedals and pumped them hard, huffing as she neared her cousin. "But…I thought…you said…this…was…it."

Lexie skidded to a stop and gave Anne the full weight of her glare. "Does this look like a town to you?"

Coming to a standstill beside her cousin, Anne studied the mammoth cedar tree they'd stopped under, its trunk the breadth of a lighthouse. "Well, no. But you said—."

"Oh, my God, you are so—. Just forget it. Let's go." Lexie was moving again, perhaps even faster than before.

Anne lost sight of her within seconds, but this time made no effort to keep up. Meandering along the trail, she breathed the forest in deep, keeping pace only with the dragonflies. The trip was dreamy, but brief. Just beyond the rise, behind which Lexie had vanished, the forest parted to reveal an overgrown clearing. There, a path of velvet-green grass lay before her like a runner. Anne's mouth gaped as she traced it to twin rows of enormous, Victorian-styles houses lining either side. There were perhaps fifteen to twenty in total, all covered in climbing vines. Their paint was worn and shingles hung like decayed husks from their bodies. But they were grand. Anne could see them as they once were — in rich, glossy coats of every color in the rainbow. She could see their bright-white flower boxes, teeming with violets and pansies. She could see their wide, airy porches freshly adorned with intricate woodwork of the finest quality.

"Beautiful. Just beautiful," she breathed.

"Hey, Sally-stares-a-lot, we're over here!" Lexie was waving from near a narrow, tan three-story home, two houses in. She stood near four other kids about her age, two girls and two boys. Anne descended the nob and made her way towards them. "So, y'all, this is my cousin, Anne," Lexie announced as Anne dropped her bike alongside the others'.

Anne kept her eyes low. "Hi," she squeaked. A cascade of "Heys," followed, though if they numbered four, she couldn't be certain.

"So, Anne…Lexie says you've never been here before, huh?" A shaggy-haired boy of perhaps sixteen was watching her with bright blue eyes. His voice was two octaves deeper than that of any boy in her grade.

"Um, no." Anne found herself studying the ground again. "Didn't even know about it until yesterday."

"It's totally epic," the second boy interjected. He was wearing a flannel wife-beater and little wisps of newly sprouted underarm hair framed the shirt like sideburns. "Totally haunted." He snickered at himself and goosed the girl he stood beside, who leapt in alarm.

"Jerk!"

"So, what's the deal anyway?" Anne asked. Her curiosity was overpowering. "Some kid I rode with on the train said a bunch of people disappeared here or something."

Shaggy moved to the front of the crowd. "Yeah, they did. Back in the Twenties. Everybody in town…all gone at once." He had kind eyes and Anne lingered on them until she felt a blush rising on her cheeks.

"So, um," Anne's head dipped again. "What happened to 'em?"

"Malaria," Shaggy rumbled. His eyes turned to stone, his face to ash.

"No, no!" Goosey-girl freed herself from Sideburns' clutches and barged towards Anne. Her shorts were so short that the pocket linings hung below the denim. "It was the Rapture! My Aunt Debbie said they were all in some big weirdo cult, or something. Said they all got whisked away to Heaven."

"Whatever, Brittany! You're so stupid!" The final girl marched over, her flaming red hair trailing behind her like a superhero cape. "And you don't know what you're talking about either, Josh. They totally abandoned the town on account of it being all haunted, and shit."

Dreamy-eyed Josh lost his cool drawl as he defended. "Oh yeah, Char? Then why'd they leave all their stuff?!"

"Duh, Josh!" Lexie railed, stepping up beside Char, "Haven't you ever seen "Amityville" or "Poltergeist," or anything scary? When people are freaked out, they just drop their shit and run!" Char gave Lexie an approving nod. Standing hands-on-hips beside one another, they resembled two-thirds of Charlie's Angels.

Sideburns joined a half-circle the group had created, dropping his backpack in the middle of it. Gaping open, the sack revealed a six-pack of beer inside. "I say they just got drunk and had a killer goin' away party," he said, a smile lighting his face.

"Bodies, man. There weren't any bodies." Josh had reverted to his husky tone. He smiled when he caught Anne watching him as he brushed a lock of hair from his face.

Lexie bent over and pulled a beer from the pack. "I say who-ever brings the beer gets to make the rules. Dane says they all went loco and offed each other. I'm cool with that." The others laughed, and a couple even patted Dane on the back as they took beers for themselves. Meanwhile, Anne's eyes climbed the grandiose house in front of which they stood, willing it to reveal its secrets. Their chatter died away as she fixed on its face and the ivy that climbed it like wrinkles.

"Anne, you want one?" Josh was nudging her, a Bud Light in each of his hands. She shook her head.

Lexie sniggered from Char's elbow. "Course she doesn't want one. Beer ain't for babies."

"I'm not a baby!"

Brittany joined the other girls, balled her fists and mimicked rubbing away tears with them. "Waaah! Not a baby, not a baby!" She sneered, revealing crooked teeth.

Anne took two stiff-legged steps towards Brittany and cast as confident a glare as she could muster. "I AM NOT A BABY."

Brittany cackled.

A pungent odor of over-applied body spray burned Anne's nostrils just as Dane appeared at her side. "Okay, then. Prove it." He held out the last of the beers, dangling it in front of her. "Crack one open like a big girl."

Anne watched the silver can swinging before her like the blade of a pendulum and found she was speechless. She'd never drunk alcohol before, but she had seen it consumed by many. It always seemed to erase common sense and lead to trouble. Her grandmother called it stupid juice. "Err…umm…" she trailed.

"Told ya. Just a widdle bitty baby," Lexie taunted in a childlike voice. She was now draped across Char's shoulder and sipping on her can, making loud slurping noises. Anne's eyes stung with the threat of tears.

"Quit raggin' on her, guys," Josh defended, sidestepping Dane, who was still wagging the beer in Anne's face. "So what? So she doesn't want a beer. That doesn't make her a baby."

Char broke from her pack, nearly sending leaning Lexie to the ground, and came at Anne like a freight train. Stepping between Anne and Josh, Char got so close that Anne could see a well-disguised pimple blooming on her upper lip. "Um, yeah, Josh. It kinda does," Char growled, her eyes narrowing as she surveyed Anne from top to bottom. "She acts like a baby. And she sure as hell looks like a baby."

"I'M NOT A BABY."

"Okay then, big-town girl…prove it." Char's eyes burned, like her fire-kissed hair. "If you won't drink, then go into one of the houses."

Lexie moved up from the foreground and perched her head on Char's shoulder. "Yeah, one of the real creepy ones!" she howled with brows tented.

Anne glanced from the beer can to the rows of houses, and back again. "Yeah, sure. I can do that. I'm not scared."

Brittany joined Char and Lexie, and the three of them took off skipping down the main road, hooting and booing along the way. A short way down, they linked hands. A low fog rolled in and curled over their footsteps, creating an eerie image for Anne to follow. The boys loped along in kind, with Dane leaping every few strides as if a rattler had bitten him. "Ooooh, you pick the house, Char. You pick it. Gotta be the rankest one!" he called ahead.

About five houses from where they began, Char slowed and then stopped suddenly. Lexie and Brittany toppled into her like falling dominos, and Char glared at the girls before turning to survey the house. "Yessss," she hissed. "This'll do nicely."

"Oh, snap!" Lexie exclaimed, maintaining a certain distance from the house. It was more run down than some of the others. The porch had all but separated from the foundation and some of the windows on the upper level bore rock-sized holes. The entire first floor was coated in a blanket of ivy so thick that Anne couldn't even see the siding. Only the door remained untouched by vines, lending the whole group a clear view of the words "DOORWAY TO NOWHERE" spray-painted across it.

"So, Big-town, still fearless?" Char was closing in again. Anne could smell her spearmint gum. Lexie trailed close behind like a devoted dog, fixed on her master. Their combined stares burrowed through Anne, sniffing out her fear. She trembled and suppressed the urge to run.

"Oh, yeah. She's scared." Lexie was eyeing her cousin now,

scrutinizing her stoic silence. "Told ya she was just a big baby."

Anne, whose eyes had been fixed on the door since she'd first read its warning, said nothing and continued to stare ahead. Her legs rooted in the ground, she watched as the door seemed to move nearer and its words seemed to grow larger. As it did so, she imagined it began to swell and pulsate like a beating heart.

"C'mon!" Lexie stepped in behind her and gave a shove.

Anne stumbled and found herself a matter of inches from the porch's bottom step by the time she'd regained her footing. She reached out and gripped the ivy-tangled handrail without realizing she'd done so. Her legs climbed the rotting steps without her permission. Her feet carried her right to the Doorway to Nowhere before she could stop them. Her ghostly, pale hand, somehow not her own, twisted the iron knob and pushed the door open wide.

"Holyyyy shit. She friggin' did it!" Based upon his volume, Dane was still a good twenty feet back from the house, but his words stung in Anne's ears as if he were screaming an inch from her face.

Char was less impressed. "Big deal. So she opened a door. Whoop-dee-doo!" Anne could hear Char approaching from the rear, the tap, tap, tap of her tennies on the stairs as she ascended them. When she spoke again, the heat from her breath tickled Anne's left ear. "Okay, big girl, let's see what you've got then. Get your ass inside."

Anne stepped inside as if dangling on marionette strings. The floorboards creaked under her weight. A wide staircase with dingy ivory steps emerged from the darkness in front of her, but she veered right and into a parlor just inside the threshold. Just as Josh had foretold, the room was fully furnished and, aside from some vandals' disarray and a thick coat of dust, just as if its owners had left for Sunday church. A floral couch with wooden legs sat at the center of the room with matching chairs positioned on each arm, the cushions missing from all of them. Indentations from the coffee table, which had once sat before them, remained in the floor but their owner lay in the hearth, only its singed claw feet remaining. A porcelain doll sat on the ground in front of the fireplace, as if an eternity of waiting had failed to warm her stony bones. Her glassy eyes stared up at the ceiling. Anne approached the toy, her hands trembling. A perfect X had been drawn over the doll's mouth.

WHAM! A thud echoed from the hallway and brought the doll to life with its vibration. Her painted eyes darkened along with the room. Rushing towards the root of the noise, Anne quickly arrived at the front door and found it closed. Pulse racing, she twisted the knob but met resistance on the opposite side. "Oh, man, oh, man, oh, man!" she sputtered, digging her heels into the floorboards and pulling with her full weight. Anne strained endlessly but felt no give. Panic swelled in her gut. "HELP! HELP ME! THE DOOR'S JAMMED!"

Muffled yet unmistakable howls of laughter echoed from beyond the door. Anne raced back to the parlor room and approached its eastern-most window, which faced the street outside. There appeared five blurry figures, growing steadily smaller as they dashed into the distance. Squinting against the filthy windowpanes, Anne could distinguish the mound of bikes as they neared it and looked on in horror as six bikes rode out of town with just five riders. Lexie wobbled, laboring to steer her bike while towing the one Anne had ridden. Or perhaps it was merriment that had her off balance.

Anne returned to the front door, hot tears streaming down her cheeks as she yanked at the knob again and again. It wouldn't give an inch. Her sobs came in spasms until she collapsed against the jam and slid into a defeated heap beneath it. The floorboards were dusty and Anne's tears pooled upon them in muddy little puddles. She watched them swell to lakes until she was dry and then sucked in a deep breath and wiped her cheeks clean.

The staircase before her beckoned and Anne rose with a mind to seek out the shattered windows she'd noticed on the second floor, and along with them, an escape route. The stairs groaned beneath her weight and she slowed to a cautious pace. As she reached the landing, Anne came upon a catwalk that had been hidden in shadow from her vantage point on the first floor. It was lined with bookshelves on one side, and as she neared it, she was pleased to see a few volumes still scattered amongst the cobwebs. A rich, red book with gold embossing caught Anne's eye and she plucked it from the stacks. "'The Crimson Fairy Book' by Andrew Lang," she read aloud, passing over the raised lettering with delicate fingertips. A musty smell wafted up from its pages as Anne cracked the book open to an illustration of a lithe little fairy riding atop the back of a barn owl. Glancing back to the bookcase, she noticed a similar sprite on the cover of another of the novels, bearing the title "The Blue Fairy Book." She gripped its spine, but as she moved to pull it from the shelf, the hollow space left behind revealed an enormous rodent who leapt directly towards her. Anne recoiled, falling backwards onto the railing behind her. Snaps of splintering wood resounded through the house as the rotted banister split and sent her plummeting towards the lower story. Time seemed to slow as she watched the dusty chandelier hanging from the ceiling sway when she impacted and broke through the floor-boards below. In an instant, all went black.

Chapter Three

When she was a young child, Anne's Uncle Mike had delighted in tickling her. She could still see his moustache twitch, revealing
a toothy grin as his hearty bellow joined with hers. She could still
feel the scratch of his worn fingertips. The sensation was remarkably
crisp: too crisp. Anne parted her eyelids, jolting at the sight of a size-
able Daddy longlegs inching up her forearm. He promptly tumbled
to the ground, and in a flash, Anne was on her feet, head whipping
wildly as she surveyed her surroundings. A swell of pain shot to her
brain and she felt mildly lightheaded. She collapsed backward onto
the pile of rubbish on which she'd first fallen and found herself staring up through a gaping hole in the ceiling. A story above, the gaudy
chandelier still sparkled beneath its fur of dust, as if laughing as her.

Once her head had leveled out, Anne returned her focus to the
room in which she'd landed. Though illuminated only by a small
shaft of light spilling in from the first floor, she could tell that this
room was unlike the others in the house. Ample furnishings stood
like sentinels in the darkness and personal effects like blankets, children's toys and dishware were peppered throughout. Clearly, vandals had not yet paid a visit. Anne rose on aching legs and tripped
over a large chest, nearly falling yet again. "Grrrrrr," she growled.

A chair and side table sat nearby and Anne drifted towards them, praying that the oil lamp outline she'd locked on in the blackness was truly what awaited her there. "FINALLY, something goes my way!" she rejoiced. A one-time Girl Scout with enough merit badges to certify herself as a nerd for all eternity, Anne fished a box of matches from a tiny drawer in the lamp's base and had the room glowing in seconds flat. Though a great many things in the newly lit space enticed her, it was the small door on the far east end that beckoned most. She nearly swore aloud as she approached and found a large brass lock hanging from its jam. "Great, now what?" she grumbled.

Anne's eyes drifted upwards again, evaluating the ten-foot height between her and the story above. She'd never make it. "Great. Guess I'll just die here," she said aloud.

A poof of dust kicked up as she settled on the floor with a huff. The mammoth trunk that had tripped her earlier sat only inches away, its keyhole hanging open like a yawning mouth. "And just what are you gawking at?" she barked, scooting nearer to inspect it. The carving on its face was like nothing she'd ever seen. Leafless trees lined the lid, their limbs curling to form wicked faces with enormous eyes and no mouths. Beneath the trees, small children played and though she could not reason why, Anne felt that the creatures buried in the branches were watching them.

Certain the trunk was locked, Anne reached towards it with low expectations and was surprised as it cracked open like a bud welcoming the sun. A child's treasure lay inside: toys and trinkets, dried flowers and a beautiful horse carved from wood. Anne withdrew the horse, gliding her hands over its smooth flanks. It wore a miniature saddle, replicated to the finest detail. Aged as the toy was, it shone as if new and Anne looked upon it warmly, imagining how prized a possession it had once been. She suddenly felt lecherous holding such a trophy and moved towards the trunk to return it. It was then that she saw the journal.

Bound in supple leather and carved with the initials G.R., the diary had as melodic a siren song as any forbidden thing could. Anne opened it.

December 27th, 1920

Mother has given me this fine journal for Christmas. She says that I would do well to write in it daily. She hopes that in writing here, my fanciful desires may be quelled and will thus aid me in becoming a pious young woman. I do wish to please her but feel more at home amongst the boys, playing in the woods, than I do attending Sunday tea. Perhaps if I am dutiful with my entries I shall learn to behave more like the lady I am meant to be.

Father seems pleased with me as I am. Today he let me join in crafting a saddle for the beautiful horse he carved. It is a glorious animal and I labor under the weight of choosing a name for it. John says I ought to call him Comanche after General Custer's horse, but I find that name dull. After all, perhaps it is a girl horse? In that case, Beauty seems a much more fitting name.

I shall write again soon, diary. At present I must join Father, Mother, John and baby Jacob in town. The New Year's celebration comes with haste and I am excited to see the banner hung.

Most sincerely yours,

Grace Rowden

Anne flipped the book closed, tracing the initials indented in its cover. She glanced towards the trunk, where the horse's head peeked above its lip, his erect ears skimming the edge like tiny shark fins. Upon rising to retrieve him, she found her joints still ached from the earlier fall: a painful reminder of the day she'd momentarily forgotten in the pages of Grace Rowden's diary.

"Hey there, horsey. Beauty, is it?" she asked. Anne lifted the toy and as she did, a glint appeared just below its belly. She squinted, laboring in the darkness, and reached cautiously inside the trunk. Fumbling between jacks and bonnets she followed the shiny object like a lure, digging deeper and deeper until it seemed as though the trunk might go on forever. Finally, pushed to tiptoes, Anne made a final stretch and seized what she'd hoped she'd seen…a key. Even in the dimness, she recognized the same brass twinkle from the lock on the room's only door. She hastened towards it, sputtering "Please, please, please!" all the way, with the key firmly in her grip.

Like a hand to a glove, the key entered its mate and Anne breathed a sigh of relief as it clicked open. She freed the lock and pulled the door ajar, though with considerable effort. Fresh air spilled into the cellar along with the dim of twilight. "Oh my God, how long have I been down here?"

A narrow stairway lay before her, but as Anne moved towards it, she hesitated. After a quiet moment in thought, she spun on her heels and sprinted towards the trunk. In seconds, she'd doused the flame on her light, collected the journal and emerged again into the tepid night. She circled to the front of the house and then made her way onto the main street. The houses were even spookier nearing night. Pale curtains fluttered in their windows, appearing like specters in her peripheral vision. Branches swayed with the breeze, casting shadowy hands that seemed to lurch at her as she passed. Nearing the last of the houses, Anne startled at a peculiar flutter above it. She lifted her eyes to the sky and puzzled over a narrow piece of cloth that she hadn't noticed there earlier in the day. After marching ahead to gain a better vantage point, Anne turned to face a loosely strung banner that read, "HAPPY NEW YEAR! Welcome, 1921!"

The hairs on the back of Anne's neck went suddenly rigid and she found her once heavy legs now nimble and willing. Curls of hot breath lit her way as she dashed along the forest path, clutching the leather diary close to her body. Beneath the cloak of dusk, underbrush grabbed at her pant legs like beastly claws. Despite Anne's love of the wood, relief surged through her as barren turf appeared in the near distance. She slowed to a trot as she approached the ring of rocks that marked the forest border, but as she moved to cross it,

Anne found she was unable.

"What the—?!" Anne collected herself and made a second attempt to step over the stones but was propelled backwards. Frozen in confusion, she stared ahead for moment before proceeding at a slower pace. Once again, a force she could neither see nor explain seemed to limit her passage. She fixed on the hollow space in front of her and then on the boulders below it. Perhaps it was the ring that confined her? After all, Lexie had claimed it was magical…however trustworthy her word was.

Anne canvassed the earth around her and promptly located a thick tree branch. She laid down Grace's journal beside it and then grabbed the limb with both hands. Notching it beneath the nearest stone, Anne bore her weight down and pushed. Grunts of effort filled the night air as she strained, scooped and jabbed, but no amount or variety of effort dislodged the rocks. Finally, in a fit of desperation, Anne made a running jab at the ring. Her spear lodged in the base of the boulders and sent her careening over the top like a pole-vaulter. Knocked breathless on the other side, it took her a moment to regain her faculties and realize she'd succeeded.

"Holy crap!" Anne jumped to her feet and scooped up her trusty tree limb. "Ha! That'll show ya!" She triumphantly waved the branch at the rocks before noticing the book she'd left behind.

"Oh, no, you don't!" she warned the rocks. Anne inched towards the ring with calculated steps and an ingenious plan. Near enough to touch it, but mindful not to, she hung her limb over the top of the rocks like a fishing pole. It took an ugly pirouette and some creative stretching, but Anne managed to snag the corner of the journal with her stick and pull it to the edge of the ring. With a shoot from the branch tucked beneath the book, Anne jimmied the book up and onto the rocks, nudging it towards her. She may as well have tried to pull a pickup truck with her teeth. The same resistance she'd met when trying to cross the ring earlier now returned in full force. Labor as she might, the journal would not budge. Turned on its top, it seemed to hover in mid-air just within her grasp, and yet it couldn't have been any further from reach. As soon as she conceded and let the limb go slack, the book toppled to the ground inside the ring. Deciding it was unwise to leave it in the open, Anne used her stick to nudge it beneath the bush near which it had fallen and bid it goodnight.

By the time she'd made the trek back to her aunt and uncle's house, the sky was black. Anne sulked past the bike that would have sped her journey home, glaring at Lexie's personalized mini license plate stuck on the back. She would have felt impolite not doing so, so she rapped on the door lightly before entering. "Hello?" As she stuck her head inside she could smell greasy food being prepared.

"What's that?" Claudia appeared in the hallway holding a frying pan. She had a cigarette between her lips and wore a floral housecoat that looked like a bed sheet. Her expression turned immediately sour when she saw Anne. "Well, then, look who it is."

Anne dipped her head and approached her aunt with eyes downcast. "I'm really sorry, Aunt Claudia. I— I—," she fumbled.

"Land's sakes, what in the world happened to you?!" Claudia pitched the pan around the corner onto the countertop and hastened towards her niece. Worry lines rutted her brow. "You look like you've been run over by a truck!" she exclaimed, scissoring Anne with her meaty arms.

"Oh…" Anne sputtered, suddenly remembering her fall and realizing she must look frightful. "I, uh—"

Lexie appeared at her mother's side as if by magic. "Looks like she fell in the gully to me. Ya know, that one over by Rather's house. That'll sneak up on ya in the dark." She glowered at Anne, her eyes three shades darker than normal. Anne nodded.

Claudia was still squeezing her niece far too tightly, the worry dents in her forehead deepening. "Well what on earth were you doin' traipsin' around in the dark anyhow? Where you been girl?"

"Well, I uh—." Anne eyeballed Lexie who was still glaring at her. "I, um…"

"Didn't you say you were going to town, Anne? Weren't you gonna hit the arcade?" Lexie's lips drew into a tight little line. Her stare turned fiery.

Anne's eyes darted from Claudia's puckered brow to Lexie's pinched lips and then back again. She knew she'd be in far more trouble if Claudia knew the truth, and of course, if she tattled, Lexie would eat her alive. "Yeah, yeah. I was headed back from the arcade. Sorry, Aunt Claudia. I didn't mean to stay so long. I was trying to beat the high score on "Mortal Kombat" and I just got distracted." She scuffed her feet at the carpet and widened her eyes. "I'm really sorry."

Claudia's face smoothed but her gaze lingered as if wooed by doubt. "Hmmm, well, okay then. So long as you don't pull nothin' like that again," she trailed, returning to the kitchen. From the other side of the wall she continued. "Oh, and your folks called. Had to feed 'em a line of bull about where you were." Suddenly her face appeared in the doorway flanking the hall. Her eyes had hardened. "Don't you ever make me lie for you again. You got it?"

"Yes, ma'am."

"Now why don't you girls set the table? Dinner'll be ready soon."

The girls gathered dishes and silverware in silence, neither looking at the other. By the time Pat wandered in from his throne in the living room, the quiet bordered on uncomfortable. "Well, nice to see you've decided to join us," he greeted Anne. She smiled sheepishly and set an empty glass in front of his plate. "Looks like you've been playin' in the woods or something."

After not hearing it for so long, Lexie's voice was shrill-sounding as she piped, "No, Dad, she fell in Rather's gully. She was walkin' home from the arcade and didn't see it in the dark." Her

43

words moved quickly, as if running from the truth. Pat only grumbled in reply.

Anne wandered off to wash up and when she returned to the table she found the rest of the family had started eating without her. Taking an empty chair in front of a mound of steaming meatloaf, she gave a gentle smile to her aunt, who still regarded her with narrowed eyes. "So, I was thinkin'," Claudia began, "I've got to head into town on errands tomorrow. And I was thinkin' it might not be such a great idea to leave you on your own." Anne muscled down a mouthful of cornflake-infused meat log and examined her plate in silence. "Anyway, I 'spose you ought to come along with me. Can't have you breakin' your neck on my clock."

"Yeah, okay." Anne mashed at her meal until it appeared she'd made a sincere attempt to eat it and asked to be excused. Retreating to Lexie's room, she quickly dressed for bed and disappeared beneath the covers. When her cousin entered several minutes later, Anne feigned sleep as Lexie went through her nighttime rituals and eventually lay down in the bed next to hers. The day's events replayed in Anne's head over and over and refused to let her rest. Reliving Lexie's betrayal as her cousin lay just beside her seemed to bring color to a vision that had previously appeared only in black and white. After endless tossing and turning, Anne sat up in bed. "Thanks a lot, Lexie," she snarled. "Real great cousin you are."

Lexie groaned beneath her blankets and turned onto her side to face the opposite direction. For a delicious moment Anne contemplated jumping atop her and screaming like a lunatic. "And nice touch with the banner. Don't know how you pulled that off. Real forethought, though. Pretty crafty. You must really hate me." Lexie grunted and buried her head beneath her pillow. Within minutes, she was snoring loudly. The rise and fall was unending. Finally, it woke the sun.

"I'm not a morning person," Lexie growled as Anne tiptoed around the room gathering her clothes.

"Oh, no? Well, then—." Anne's soft footsteps turned to thuds as she pulled on her shoes and sloppily made her bed. Slamming the door closed behind her, she gained a supremely satisfied grin.

A tinkling of cereal falling on plastic called from the kitchen and Anne arrived there to find Claudia fresh-faced and holding a bowl out to her. "This'll be fun," she'd decided. "Lexie never wants to go anywhere with me. We'll have a girls' day." Claudia had a freshly applied coat of hot pink lipstick on and, together with her signature baby-blue eye shadow, she was a shoe-in for Barnum & Bailey. Anne only smiled and accepted her breakfast.

Bellies full and buckled in Claudia's minivan, Anne learned that amongst her aunt's errands were a trip to the nail salon and the beauty parlor. A troubling reference to waxing accompanied the latter and suddenly Lexie's company didn't seem so distasteful. "Umm, I've got some summer reading to do," Anne fibbed. "Maybe while you're doin' that stuff I could go to the library? Woodland's got one, right?"

"Now why would you wanna go to the library?" Claudia jogged her head like a rooster. "Didn't ya hear me, girl? We're goin' to the salon!" A little sparkle illuminated her eyes as she spoke her final word.

"No, no. It sounds really cool. And I'd totally love to go." Anne returned with forced enthusiasm. "It's just that I don't wanna get behind. And I think I left one of the books I need back at home." Claudia's smile dipped to a scowl and Anne could sense her digging in. "I umm…I don't wanna flake out on my reading. If I get a bad grade in English again, my folks are gonna be really mad."

"Oh." Claudia fumbled. "Well, we don't want that. I don't wanna be the cause of that. Goodness knows, I've got enough to answer to with your folks already."

"Yeah. It stinks. Just the way it goes, I guess." Anne turned towards the window and shared a smirk with her reflection. Beyond her double, green trees faded to brown shingles as they entered downtown. Claudia pulled up aside a stately brick building with gridded windows and parked.

"You sure this is where you wanna go?"

"Totally." Anne hopped out of the van and climbed the stone steps to the library, waving to her aunt as the van drove out of sight.

A familiar musk hung in the library's foyer, and it grew stronger as Anne approached the main desk. An antique woman with cat's eye spectacles sat there, her nose buried in "Pride and Prejudice." She didn't look up from the book as she asked, "May I help you?"

"Well, I'm not sure," Anne admitted. "I'm looking for a book, but I don't know what it's called."

"Mm." The woman raised her eyes from novel, its jacket still hiding the lower part of her face. "Well, then, just what would this book be about?"

Anne glanced nervously about the lobby. They were alone. "Umm…well…a town."

"And the name of this town?"

"Well…umm…that's the thing." Anne's eyes got big. "I don't really know that, either."

The librarian made a heavy sigh, placed a scrap of paper in her book and set it on the counter. "I see," she said, leveling her gaze at Anne. "Then just how am I meant to help you, miss?" Her mouth was straight as an arrow.

"I was thinking—err…hoping—that you might know the name." Anne rung her hands and conjured the best doe eyes she could emulate. "I've only ever heard people call it Nowhere Town."

The librarian stiffened in her chair, the skin on her face drawn tight like a rubber mask. She canvassed the lobby just as Anne had done, only to find it empty. Leaning across the desk, her eyeglass chains skimmed its top and then coiled beneath her as she stopped just inches from Anne's face. "Well, you know why they call it that, don't you?" she hissed.

Anne shook her head, the remainder of her body frozen.

The librarian leaned in even closer, her eyes silver dollars beneath the glasses. "They call it that because it has no name. Or if it did, no one wanted to remember." She pushed the glasses up tight to the bridge of her nose, and continued: "And you won't find and books about it here, if there ever were any."

"But why?" Anne asked at a whisper.

"On account of the disappearance, I suppose." The librarian's eyes jumped from one end of the building to the other, as if watching a tennis match. Finding it still vacant, she explained, "Folks just don't like to talk about that. They're scared of what they can't explain."

Revisiting the stories of Lexie's friends, Anne cocked her head sideways and asked, "So no one really does know what happened to the townspeople?"

"Not with any real certainty. Of course, one person will tell you their great uncle's half-brother's best friend witnessed the whole ordeal, and recounted it on down to them as the God's truth, but no one really knows."

A creak echoed from the foyer, and both Anne and her informer jerked their heads towards it. Wearing Bermuda shorts and a wide grin, a teenaged boy ascended the stairs with a newspaper in hand. "Hello, Mrs. Engleburtson," he greeted as he approached them. He handed the rolled paper across the desk to her, and added, "Today's paper, right on schedule."

"Thank you kindly, Zach," she said with a nod and a short demeanor.

Zach caught Anne's roaming eyes and curled his lip. "Hey."

"Hey."

A heavy satchel hung across Zach's shoulder and he readjusted it with a huff. "Okay. Well, then, see you tomorrow," he said. His flip-flops clapped against the tile floors as he exited, leaving them alone once again.

Anne refocused herself on the librarian, whom she realized had actually shared very little. Mrs. Engleburtson had laid the paper aside and was quietly tending her nose with an embroidered handkerchief. "So, do you know anything else? I mean anything with real certainty?" Anne asked.

Ms. Engleburtson raised one eyebrow and turned down her nose. "I know a great many things, my child. And indeed, many of them with absolute certainty!"

"Sorry. About the town. I just wondered if you knew anything more about the town." Anne batted her eyes and dipped her head. "I was just really hoping to learn more."

"Well, I can tell you this, they weren't well liked, the people of that little village. Times were tough back in those days. A lot of families around here didn't make it. And yet in that village, everything prospered, everything grew…and those folks didn't seem inclined to share it."

Anne perched her elbows on the desk and cupped her chin in her palms. "Wonder why."

"Difficult to say," Mrs. Engleburtson returned. "I suppose in those times people took care of their own. Perhaps that's why they kept to themselves like they did. Perhaps that's why the town is such a mystery."

Softly nodding, Anne fell quiet, as did the librarian. In the great hollow of the library, the silence was amplified. "Well, thank you," Anne finally whispered. "Thank you for sharing what you know."

Mrs. Engleburtson nodded and reached for her novel as Anne followed the scent of musty pages into the belly of the building, filled with more questions than ever.

Amidst the warm embrace of the stacks, Anne trailed her pointer finger across spines of familiar titles, not really knowing what she was looking for. She sought out the History section, but no magical books with forbidden secrets revealed themselves. Selecting "Woodland: A History in the Trees" from its nook on the shelf, she landed a chair nearby and set to sleuthing. The book was dry and Anne found herself skipping most of the text, focusing instead on the black-and-white photos that peppered its pages. Sullen faces haunted the pictures of weathered men gathered around fallen trees and sawmills. Dreary women in full-length dresses held infants who looked somber even in their youth.

"I heard you asking about the town." A voice crackled, startling

Anne, who nearly dropped the heavy book laid across her lap. She whipped her head left and right, seeking it source, but no one appeared.

"Hello?"

A slow, steady creak registered from the shadows two stacks over. In the dimness, the crumpled figure of a man rose from a chair that had been camouflaged by darkness. Heavy with age, he made his way towards her with noticeable effort. He carried a cane fashioned from a lacquered tree limb and his face hung in saggy, wrinkled bags. "I say, I heard you askin' about that town," he repeated. Even his lips moved slowly.

"Oh, yes." Anne stumbled. "Do you know it?"

"I suppose." He bobbed his head and studied her with his milky eyes. "My older brother, Artie, had a friend who lived there."

"Oh, really?" Anne perked up and leaned forward. "Can you tell me anything about it? Like what happened there?"

The old man was still bobbing, seemingly without control. "Ah, no, not really. I was just a baby back when all that happened."

"Oh," Anne breathed, deflated.

"Ah, well, I 'spose I'm not entirely useless though." He steadied on his cane and dipped down low. "Weren't you askin' for the name? The name of the town?"

Anne lifted her head level to his. "Well, yeah, but I thought it didn't have one."

He smiled, and his face contorted into a dried turnip. "I only know it by the name Artie used to call it. Back then they called it Devlin."

Anne inched nearer. "Why'd they call it Devlin?"

"Well, child, they called it that because the Devil lived in there."

Chapter Four

Following her discoveries in the library, Anne vowed never again to return to Devlin. She became a dutiful helpmate to Claudia and even went fishing with her Uncle Pat a few times. She and Lexie worked out routines that helped them to avoid one another, and though her days were long and mundane, she found comfort in their safety.

"So, you think this fish will be as hard to cook as it was to catch?" Pat asked. He dropped a foot-long trout on the kitchen counter, which created a distasteful squishing noise.

Anne shrugged her shoulders just as Claudia arrived in the doorway behind her and bellowed, "What the hell is that nasty fish doing on my kitchen counter?" She marched towards her husband and kicked him in the shin, following which Pat whimpered and clutched his leg before slinking away like a wounded animal.

"Oh, no, you don't. Somebody's gotta clean this thing and it sure as hell isn't gonna be me!" Claudia barked at his heels. Little to either of their surprise, Pat had already vanished.

"Looks like I'm your gal," Anne conceded. She pulled a knife from the drawer and hooked the fish by its gills with her fingertips.

Claudia suddenly drew her hands up as if she'd seen a spider. "Oh, God, I can't watch," she exclaimed, and promptly shuffled out of the room, her derriere jiggling like a Jell-O mold as she went.

Anne cringed as a wave of tiny eggs spilled from the fish as she slit its belly open. They pooled in a gelatinous heap in the kitchen sink and she tried not to look at them while degutting their limp mother. When footsteps approached from the hall, Anne relished the opportunity to turn her nose from the odious stench of fish guts.

"Oh, yeah, totes. Meetchya there at 10." Lexie appeared just behind her voice, lowering a phone from her ear. She scrunched her nose as she walked in and then glared at Anne. "Aw, nasty!"

The fish suddenly seemed less off-putting and Anne resumed gutting it. Behind her, Lexie collapsed in one of the dining chairs with a thump. "So…looks like we found your little playpen," Lexie mocked. She was sneering as Anne turned to face her.

"What are you talking about?"

Lexie curled a lock of her hair around her pointer finger and snapped her gum, still grinning wickedly. "In Nowhere Town. Brittany and Dane, they found your little secret room." Lexie snorted a half-laugh. "I always wondered how you got outta that house."

Anne returned to her task, saying nothing.

"We're gonna go out there tomorrow," Lexie continued, "Gonna see if we can find anything good. Maybe sell some shit, make some money." She rose to leave, pausing just behind Anne as she departed. "Hope the baby won't miss any of her toys."

Lexie's snide comment stuck in Anne's head, reverberating there for the balance of the evening. Even as she lay in bed willing herself to sleep, the cellar room kept returning to her. Images of Lexie and her friends pilfering the beautiful trunk and its trove of treasures played in her mind over and over until they'd sickened her. By the time the light of sunrise came, Anne knew what she must do.

Lexie, who was snoring like a grizzly bear, didn't rouse as Anne quietly dressed and gathered her things. She tiptoed through the trunk of the house and found it still and alien, dawn's dim light casting shadows where there were normally none. After leaving a carefully written lie behind, Anne crept outside and approached Lexie's two bikes while wearing a malicious grin. Their tires moaned with sweet release as she relieved them of air. "That oughta do it," she decided, rising from the deflated bike and erecting its untouched brother.

The hour was still early, and even in mid-July the air was crisp and cool. Anne retraced the path that she and Lexie had made weeks ago, but this time an unsettled gut accompanied her on the ride. Unpleasant as it was, Anne preferred it to the company of her cousin. When she neared the forest border, her new riding companion willed her to retreat but determination drove her forward. When she finally skidded to a stop at the rock ring, her stomach made an audible groan.

Anne had seen the ring in distorted forms so many times in her dreams that the real thing now appeared almost harmless. Studying the small stones, she began to question the validity of her memories, now so old and corroded. "I wonder if…" she trailed, sidestepping along the boulder border until she faced a small bush that lay just on the other side. From under its head of waxy green leaves, a sliver of leather peeked through. Acting on instinct, Anne reached for it and stepped over the ring in the process. She gasped as her foot touched enchanted soil. It was too late now.

The journal was a little damp, but otherwise unharmed by its stay of several weeks in the wild. Anne placed it gingerly in her knapsack and elected to walk the rest of the way to Devlin. She wasn't yet prepared for what might happen if she tried to cross the threshold to retrieve her bike.

Without Lexie to rush her journey, Anne ambled along the forest path. The sun had fully risen and shafts of light punctured the evergreen canopy like laser beams. Many of the trees were enormous, stretching hundreds of feet into the sky. On a nature walk in the Olympic National Forest, her father had once told her, "Trees grow years, not feet. They age to the heavens." Anne marveled at the skyscrapers now, feeling the weight of her dad's words. These trees had looked on as Devlin was built. They had watched as the town grew and prospered; surely, they'd witnessed its demise. What secrets they must hold.

The emerald-flocked ridge concealing Devlin appeared in the near distance like a velvet curtain about to part for a grand performance. Anne pushed down the knot in her gut and climbed the hill to meet it. On the other side, the town glittered with the glow of day-break, somehow softer than she'd remembered. The ivy ensnaring several of the houses fluttered its leaves at her as she passed, seemingly in welcome. She canvassed the hollow faces of the homes, each one the same but somehow different. When she arrived in front of the ominous home with the leaning porch, Anne was surprised to find it less eerie than she'd recalled. The crooked porch, like an old man's sagging mouth, gave it a distinct character that the other houses did not possess. Its shattered upper windows held near-identical stars of missing glass, and Anne proclaimed to the curmudgeonly face, as she set off on the side yard, "You've got stars in your eyes."

One of the cellar doors was ajar, the lock she'd removed still hanging from its latch. Anne peeked inside and listened as her hello bounced off the walls inside. "Guess nobody's home," she decided. "Thank God."

Sun spilled in from the first-floor windows and through Anne's self-made skylight, landing squarely on the chest. She hastened towards it and was elated to find all its original contents intact. Anne removed the delicate wooden horse along with a few other trinkets of note and began stuffing them in her pack. It was a tight fit and removing the journal allowed all the puzzle pieces to come together just right. Anne had been dreaming of the journal since it left her hands and as she let it fall open, the urge to read was irresistible.

January 21st, 1921

It is dreadfully cold this month. We remain houseguests with the Miller family whilst Father continues the work on what is to be our new home. He tells us nightly of its progress and the craftsmanship with which he and the other men labor. I am eager to see my new room, which Mother says will be all my own. At present, I must lie nightly beside Nelly Miller, who snores in her sleep and stinks of cabbage. She says we are like sisters. I do not have the heart to tell her otherwise.

As I write, Father has arrived home. He has laid the final board on the first floor. We shall be home soon!

Anne struggled to distinguish the next of Grace's passages as darkness swallowed the beams of light that had illuminated the journal's pages just moments before. She rubbed at her eyes and glanced around at the encroaching black. Had the sun vanished? Anne tipped her head back and gaped at the solid ceiling that appeared overhead as if by magic. Covered by the fresh floorboards from Grace's journal, the hole was no more. Her heart throbbed and her breath quickened.

Anne rose to her feet slowly. She began inching towards the exit just as a trail of voices floated through it. They were growing louder, closer. Straining, she picked Lexie's from amongst the clatter. Though several of her cousin's words were inaudible, Anne recognized her own name when it was mentioned, along with a reference to "ass whoopin'." She'd backed several feet from the open doorway when a glint from the lock still hanging on its handle tugged at her.

The onslaught was near now. Char's words were crisp as they drifted into the bowels of the cellar. "Waddya wanna bet me she's down there playing dress up with some dollies?" Peals of laughter followed, flooding the room.

Anne hurried up the steps and pulled the heavy wooden doors shut as quietly as she could manage. In the dark she'd created, little else was visible beyond the golden lock that swung there like a firefly in the night. Anne linked it through the handles and backed down the stairs in silence. Fixed on the exit, she cupped her mouth as the doors rattled, the lock bouncing in kind. Watching the lock as it trembled, it occurred to her how curious it was that the cellar locked from the inside.

"What the hell? It's locked!" She recognized Dane's pubescent clangor in an instant.

"You're just not pulling hard enough." Char's raspy tone was similarly unforgettable. "Just get outta the way."

The doors fell momentarily still, only to quake more violently upon their second eruption. Anne tightened the grip over her mouth, suppressing a small yelp.

Abruptly, the tremors stopped, followed by a grumble from Char. "Whatever. This is dumb, anyway. Let's get outta here and go to Dave's. I could totally go for a burger."

"Noms!" Dane squealed.

"Yeah, alright." Disappointment laced Lexie's words as she

conceded. Surely she'd been relishing her revenge all morning. Her footsteps fell heavily as Anne listened to their retreat and when Lexie's voice came again it was distant, though no less vengeful. "Hey, guys! Wait! What about the hole? We could totally get in through there."

Sneakers pounded down the yard. Anne listened as they trickled in over her head, four sets coming to rest directly at the center of the room. The voices were far too muffled now to decode, but notably heated, nonetheless. Anne stayed tense as they railed for several minutes, relaxing only when the pitter-patter of departing footsteps echoed down to her ears.

Anne fumbled in the darkness but sought out and lit the oil lamp with reasonable ease. The room seemed to warm instantly, now cast in the light of a haven. Freshly illuminated, Anne examined the boards overhead which were rough-sawn, as if they'd just been cut. She breathed in and the tang of fresh pine filled her lungs. "But how could it…?" she trailed before shifting her focus to the cellar door, which now felt more friend than foe. "Best not to chance it. Better wait a while to make sure they're gone."

Seating herself near the trunk, Anne picked up the journal she'd discarded there. The leather cover warmed at her touch. She pulled it open and let the pages fall where they may.

April 28th, 1922

What a glorious day! I write to you at a late hour, dear diary, for today was so filled with frivolity that I had time for little else.

My thirteenth birthday was the best celebration yet. Mother gave me an exquisite brooch once worn by my great-grandmother, and Father made the most beautiful chest I've ever laid eyes on. It was made from the wood of a tree cut from The Faerie Mound, and its carvings tell the story of our town. It is somehow enchanting and frightening, all at once. Father says I am to keep it close to me, but I must confess I am somewhat unsettled at the sight of it beside me, even now.

After opening my gifts, Father and Mother announced a special treat! After receiving so many compliments on her baking, Mrs. Roddenback finally opened a Sweet Shop in her parlor. We walked to the end of town after supper and John and I picked out our favorite sweets. Mrs. Roddenback makes the most delicious fudge in all of Washington, and I knew that must be my choice. John got a thumbprint of marzipan but later asked to trade for a sliver of my fudge. To his dismay, I'd already eaten the lot!

Your friend,

Grace

Anne closed the journal, set it aside, and crawled toward the trunk. She looked at the gnarled faces embedded in the trees carved there. They looked back. Rising to her feet, she circled to the rear of the trunk, where vast fields of giant wheat reeds blanketed the panel. Though her mind assured her it was not possible, Anne saw them swaying. The hairs on the back of her neck stood on end as she backed away. Journal in hand, she grabbed her backpack and made her way towards the exit, trying her best not to look back at the trunk as she did so.

Mid-day approached and as Anne stepped into it, the sun warned that her time was fleeting. She glanced at the grassy road leading out of town and then at the book in her hand. Surely, a few more minutes wouldn't hurt. After all, a century-year-old sweet shop was calling her name.

A grey squirrel with a full, bushy tail scuttled in front of Anne and led the way. She followed him past eight or nine towering Victorian homes all dilapidated and engulfed in vegetation. She felt certain she'd know the right house when they came upon it.

"NO WAY!" Anne suddenly raced towards a midnight-blue beauty that was flanked by a picket fence. Much like its neighbors, the house was in ruin, shingles askew and suffocating in ivy. However, one portion of the house shined, as if new. The parlor window, its glass glittering against the noonday sun, was trimmed in fresh white paint. As Anne neared it, a long glass case revealed itself just inside.

Anne's new squirrel friend seemed just as intrigued as she and hopped the porch steps in three great leaps. He approached the window and stood on his back legs, stretching to peek inside.

"Whatchya see?" Anne asked. She craned over the porch rail,

and as the contents of the case came into view, her jaw dropped a solid inch. Inside, two chocolate layer cakes and a trio of pies accompanied a silver platter overflowing with a decadent array of cookies. All appeared as fresh as if they'd just been pulled from the oven. On a second tier, rows of chocolates, divinity, fudge and marzipan fell in a rainbow of rich colors.

Anne stumbled backward, nearly falling. She balled her fists and rubbed her eyes, hard. A repeat inspection found the window front still gleaming, the confections still sumptuous. She spun on her heels and she ran. She ran as if a murderer pursued her. She ran until her lungs stung. She ran like a hunted animal all through the woods, until, within footsteps of the ring, her side ached so sharply that she finally slowed.

Anne glanced back at the path she'd hammered, just as a small butterfly fluttered into view. Joined by a metallic dragonfly, the two dodged the shafts of sunlight that filtered through the tree canopy. The peace was palpable. Anne's body eased. She approached the round rocks at a creep.

"Here goes nothin'." Anne lifted her right foot over the stony line as if testing frigid water. To her surprise, it fell squarely upon the earth on the opposite side without a shred of resistance. Yet as her left foot moved to follow, there was a bothersome tug, like a schoolyard bully pulling at her pigtails. Chancing a look behind her, Anne found her backpack hovering off her shoulder blades, suspended on the Devlin side of the rocks as if by magic. She shed it as if it were aflame and watched as it fell inside the ring just as she stumbled out.

Anne grumbled to herself and then uncovered her trusty tree limb from the day prior. Still too wary to chance reentering the ring, she used the branch to drag the pack into hiding from the opposite side, and after doing, so felt oddly at ease. "Guess I'm just getting used to this stuff," she decided.

Late afternoon approached, and as Anne canvassed the bare ground outside the ring and found Lexie's bike missing, she knew she'd be hard pressed to make it back to her aunt and uncle's house by the time promised in her note. Her legs, though warmed, were weary and put up a fight as she resumed a sprint. Halfway to her destination, they grew insufferably heavy and she was forced to make up the remainder her journey at a walk.

Upon entering the house, Anne found Claudia holding a wooden spoon dripping with red sauce and staring at the clock. "Cuttin' it pretty close, kid," she ribbed, elbowing her niece. Droplets of sauce fell to the floor like apocalyptic rain.

"Sorry. I got a little turned around on the hike. Had to do some backtracking." Anne's lie sounded even better out loud than it had in her head. She added a smug smile as Claudia nodded and returned to a large silver pot heating on the stovetop. After a couple hours of labor, it produced a three-bean chili that Claudia claimed could "burn your nose-hairs off" with a mere whiff. Anne sat across from Lexie at the dinner table, choking her helping down and debating whether or not her cousin's stare was hotter than the swill her aunt had cooked up.

"So, Lex, what'd you get up to today?" Pat's eyes were watering as he swallowed his second spoonful with a labored gulp. Beads of sweat dappled his temple.

Lexie hadn't touched her meal. "Oh, not much," she replied, staring daggers at Anne. "Went down to True Value. Had to buy a tire pump."

Pat set his spoon down, sucked in a breath of cool air and wiped his brow. "What for?"

"Oh, seems somebody messed with my bike…let all the air outta the tires." Lexie was still staring. Anne's temperature rose with her spoon.

Claudia was noisily slurping up the final remnants of her bowl. It seemed she was immune to cayenne. "Wonder who the hell'd do that."

"Me, too," Lexie hissed, drawing her mouth into an unpleasant pucker.

"Well, that couldn't have taken ya all day," Pat added. This was the most talkative he'd been since Anne's arrival. When he turned his nose from the curls of spicy steam rising in front of him, his new-found motivation to engage his daughter was obvious. "What else did you and your hooligan friends get into?"

For the first time since being seated, Lexie looked away from her cousin. "Not much, really." Her head dipped and her voice took on a childish quality as she continued. "Hey Daddy, have you heard of anyone doin' work out there in that old abandoned town? Like fixin' the houses up or anything?"

Pat's brows bunched so closely together that they merged into one. "No. Now why would you be askin' a thing like that? You and your dumb-ass friends weren't out there messin' around, were you?" He leaned across the table, his formidable shadow eclipsing the cauldron of molten chili steaming at its center.

"Oh, no. No, Daddy. I wouldn't—" Lexie sputtered, her eyes drooping. For a moment, she looked genuinely afraid, but of what Anne could not be certain. Later that night in her room, all guise of innocence faded as Lexie shut and locked the door behind her. "You do realize that I'm going to have to murder you, right?"

"Look, I'm sorry. I know that wasn't cool...the whole thing with your tires." Anne fished her purse from the floor near where she slept and located her wallet inside. Emptying what remained of her summer spending money on Lexie's mattress she said, "Here. For the tire pump."

Struck silent, Lexie wandered over and scooped up the cash. She buried it deep in the back of her dresser drawer like a dog would his coveted bone and asked, "You didn't do that thing, did you? The thing with the floor boards?" When she turned to face Anne, the fear from the dinner table had returned to her face.

"Nope."

Lexie crawled across her bed on all fours, towards where Anne was still standing. "But you were there, right? You saw it?" Her pupils doubled in size.

Anne nodded, folding her arms across her chest. "Oh, yeah. I saw it alright."

Lexie pulled her legs from underneath her and then near her chest until she sat on the bed in a tightly wound ball. Peering upwards at Anne, she was like a small child watching something wondrous. "Aren't you freaked?"

Anne got quiet, panning the room. When her focus returned to Lexie, the girl before her seemed somehow smaller. "No. Not anymore."

"You aren't gonna go back, are you?"

"Yeah, I think I am. I kinda feel like I'm supposed to."

Chapter Five

Early the following morning, Anne scribbled a note about a forgotten hoodie and lit out before anyone had awoken. Sidestepping Lexie's bikes as though they were venomous, she loped along the potholed road to the forest with anticipation and newfound confidence aiding each stride. Upon approach, the wood seemed to rise up and welcome her. Inside the ring, she scooped her pack from its hiding spot in the bushes and slid the journal from an outer pocket. During her numerous sleepless hours the night prior, Anne had decided to return to the heart of town and read the diary there, in hopes that she might glimpse something magical. Halfway down the forest trail, her anticipation got the better of her and she cracked the journal, slowed her pace and walked as she read.

February 10th, 1921

John has been apprenticed to William Bailey, the chimney sweep. If he were a filthy child before, he is now intolerably so. Mother must wash his trousers three and often four times to clean them of soot. Today he arrived home carrying a baby raven in the crook of his arm. So coal-black were his clothes that I nearly did not see the fool bird!

As accounted by John, he came upon a nest while cleaning Mrs.

Habbersham's chimney. The nest was empty, save one small raven, no bigger than a plum. William Bailey informed Mrs. Habbersham of her squatter, but she had a horrible chill and wanted a fire lit just then. Mr. Bailey told John, "This goose shall cook!" and went along to light the hearth. Of course, John, being an odd duck himself, snatched that little bird right from its nest and brought it to roost here! Mother was furious when first she saw a wild creature in her home, but it has shown an affection for Jacob and won her heart in that way. It now sits aside him in his crib. I cannot believe such a thing!

John has called the bird Onyx, a name I quite like. I shall never tell him that though.

Endearingly yours,

Grace Rowden

Anne raised her head as Grace's entry ended and narrowly escaped walking into the crest that swelled at Devlin's inlet. Just above the ridge she could see a ribbon of white fluttering with the breeze. "HAPPY NEW YEAR! Welcome, 1921!" The banner was still slightly eerie, perhaps more so now that she no longer suspected Lexie and her friends of stringing it. Anne gawked as she passed underneath it, startling as a large, glossy raven flew overhead and perched nearby. Its head jerked sideways as it followed her movements. As Anne continued on and the distance between them grew, the bird took flight again, soaring in a straight line over her head before coming to rest on the nearby rooftop of a faded three-story that leaned slightly to the left. There, his mystique grew along with the puffs of grey smoke that engulfed him.

"Oh, my," Anne breathed. The chimney, growing like a tall, crooked branch from an equally twisted trunk, piped ashy clouds all around the raven as if a fresh fire warmed its belly. The bird's black eyes fixed squarely upon Anne, shining like marbles in the haze. "You've gotta be kid—. Is it—? Are you...? Onyx?"

The massive raven leapt from his spot on the roof and sailed to the ground near her feet. He approached at a waddle, his head ticking from side to side as he did. Anne crouched and outstretched her hand. So smooth, his feathers felt like water running beneath her fingers as she stroked him. She grinned. She'd never touched magic before.

Onyx hopped behind Anne as she continued through town. Bypassing the cellar room, she set her sights on Mrs. Roddenback's window of delectable wonders. Dawn was still breaking, and the dim that hung in the air was starkly offset by the bright light spilling from the sweet shop. A pool of saliva gathered in Anne's mouth as she took a second eyeful of the sinful treats that lie inside. Her initial shock at the sight had prevented her from examining the plumpness of the truffles, the golden flakes lifting from the piecrusts. She should've eaten breakfast before leaving.

Much to her chagrin, Anne found the door to Mrs. Roddenback's home locked, although noting the ivy that had made its way under the threshold left her little desire to consume anything that came from inside. She plopped down on the bottom-most step of the porch and it creaked beneath her. "Well, Onyx," she announced as the bird ambled over, "I guess we'll just have to work on waking up this town with empty stomachs!"

Anne leafed through the journal, until she'd located the spot at which she'd left off. The page had an odd texture to it, as if it had gotten wet and dried over time.

March 12th, 1921

Today we've learned that Tobias Smith is to be this year's Spring Bounty offering. Mrs. Smith is heartsick. Mr. Smith has told Father that he is honored. Tobias was chosen several weeks ago, and the family has been making their preparations. Were it me, I would not want to know until the Mound opened up to swallow me.

Tobias and I have been in school together since I was but five. One day, during our reading lesson, I was charged to recite aloud, but had forgotten my book. Tobias snuck his own copy to me whilst teacher was turned to the chalkboard. He is a kind boy and I wish very much that he were not leaving us. Why couldn't William Stanley have been chosen? He is such a despicably mean boy.

It is John's seventh year and Mother says it is time for him to learn the way of our town and the grace of our Bounty. In the cold morning hours, she sat upon his bed and told him of the Faerie. John exclaimed aloud as she retold the story of the bargain made between our ancestors and the Faerie King, to dwell within the Bounty of the ring in exchange for one human child every spring. John claims to have seen the Faerie faces watching him from the trees, as he played in the wood last summer. I suspect he lies. He wishes to seem a man, accustomed to such things. When the Faerie comes to take Tobias into the Mound and assumes his place, I fear John will not be so bold.

Mother tells John of the Bounty within the ring and explains that, without it, we would surely perish like those in neighboring towns. John says that he understands. I do not. I weep as I think of Tobias. I weep as I think that I may one day see one of my brothers in his place. And I weep as I think of the Faerie that would become my kin.

Sorrowfully yours,

Grace Rowden

Anne dropped the open book in her lap. "This can't be real." She glanced at Onyx, mirroring the befuddlement with which he'd been watching her. His head ticked to the side as Anne's mouth closed slowly, like a drawbridge being pulled up with great labor. She shrugged her shoulders, and added, "But then again, I am talking to a ninety-something-year-old raven," before she flipped the diary's page.

March 20th, 1921

72

The ceremony of the Spring Bounty was held today. As it was John's first year attending, Mother insisted that I accompany the family and offer him comfort. I wished very much to remain at home this year. I could not bear to watch Tobias disappear into the Mound, but Mother said to not attend would be disrespectful and may cast light upon us. I did abide. I've no wish to woo the attention of the Faerie.

Mother carried Jacob and Father and I held John's hands as Pastor Conner spoke the incantation to open the Portal. Before he began, I warned John of the hideousness of the creature that would emerge.

Pastor Conner is a large man with a full beard that swayed with a strange wind as he recited:

Folk of the Wood

Who have given us prosper

We call to you now

With our child to offer –

A peculiar girl suddenly appeared in the street like an apparition. She charged towards Anne, shouting, "Stop it! Stop reading!" with a wild look in her eyes. Anne startled and dropped the journal at her feet, where the girl snatched it up and darted backwards, her knee-length frock swaying under a lace apron. Her hair was as black as the raven, and as Onyx imitated her and stopped at her side, he looked to have dropped straight from her inky mane.

"What the—?" Who the heck are you?!"

The girl scooped Onyx up and cradled him in her arms like a baby. "Oh, you great silly bird! How I've missed you!" The raven laid his head back and quivered with excitement, chortling madly.

"Hello? Did you hear me?" Anne glared sideways at the bird, his alliances so easily shifted. "Who are you? Where'd you come from?"

Both girl and bird settled, granting Anne their attentions. "Well, I'd expect you would know. You must know all about me," the girl replied, dangling the journal before her like meat on a hook. "You have been reading my diary, after all."

Anne backed up the stairs on all fours like a crab. She didn't stop until the ivy curled around Mrs. Roddenback's doorjamb tickled the nape of her neck. "But she's—but you're—you're...you're Grace?" she stammered.

"It would seem that way." The girl tented her dress and made a curtsy. "Pleased to make your acquaintance." She added a kind sort of smile, then said, "And you are Anne."

Anne acknowledged with only a dumb nod.

"I've been watching you...watching the town come alive as you read. It's quite magical, isn't it?"

Anne nodded a second time.

Grace approached, though slowly. "There's no need for fear.

I don't believe it's the dark sort." She stopped as Anne stiffened against Mrs. Roddenback's front door.

"Do…do…do you know that because you're a ghost?" Anne stuttered, the ivy poking through strands of her hair as if rooting there.

"I'm not a ghost!" Grace exclaimed. Her round, ivory face puckered and then fell flat. "Or at least I don't think I am." She glanced down at the raven, still saddled in the crook of her arm, and gave him a woeful look. "I must look a fright, mustn't I, Onyx?"

"Oh, no," Anne soothed, still stumbling. "You look perfectly fine. Pretty, even." She stood and then crossed the porch's threshold with slow steps. "It's just that, well, how could you be Grace Rowden and not be a ghost? I mean," she trailed, calculating, "you'd be like a hundred and something years old by now."

Grace had been stroking and cooing at Onyx, but stopped abruptly and looked up. "What year is it?"

Anne walked towards the steps and began making her way down. "It's 2013."

Grace's choke rattled the still air. She fell to her knees, nearly pitching Onyx to the ground and then sobbed and clutched him while rocking back and forth. The bird glanced wildly about but never abandoned his mistress.

"It's alright. It's okay," Anne soothed, as she approached and laid her hand upon Grace's back. She patted and rubbed in a circular motion, as her mother often did for her when she was upset, meanwhile noting that Grace's back was neither cold nor ghostly. Grace sobbed for a time, her body gradually twitching less and less. When it seemed she'd run herself dry, Anne lowered her face to Grace's and added, "You know, it's not that bad. We've got movies and microwaves and Internet and all kinds of cool stuff that you couldn't get back in the Twenties."

Grace looked up with red-rimmed eyes and smiled. "I've no idea what any of those things are, but I'm sure they're quite lovely." She deposited Onyx on the ground in between them and he hopped off, surely glad to no longer be her feathered teddy bear.

Anne lowered to the ground and perched forward on her elbows. "I still don't get it though. If you're not a ghost, and you're not a zillion years old…what are you? Immortal or something?" Visions of fantasy films she'd seen over the years zinged through her brain, each one more enchanting than the last.

"I suppose I don't know," Grace admitted. "The very last thing I recall is Father sending me to that infernal cellar and bidding me remain in the trunk." Her face was inches from Anne's and up close, trails of dried tears shone on her cheeks. "I so wanted to do as I was told but it became unbearably difficult to breathe in such tight quarters, so after a time I crawled out. But then all went dark and there was nothing. Nothing until you read me back out." Her dry eyes linked with Anne's. "Thank you. Thank you, Miss Anne."

A smile tugged at the corners of Anne's mouth. In all her years, no one had ever called her "Miss," nor expressed such heartfelt thanks to her. "Aw, it was nothin'," she replied, dipping her head just as Onyx skittered by them, his feathers still mussed from being clutched too tightly. Anne studied the bird as he passed Mrs. Roddenback's parlor window and then turned again to Grace. "So, you've watched…seen all this weird stuff happening?"

"Indeed." Grace was staring at the sweet shop, as well. Glints of sunlight played across her eyes and set them aglow. "I looked on as you raised our New Year's banner," she added with a brilliant smile.

"And opened the sweet shop?" Anne asked while watching her new friend with amusement.

Grace grinned wider, still staring at Mrs. Roddeback's window. "Yes, and the splendid sweet shop."

"I don't get it though. Why didn't you say anything? Why didn't you reveal yourself?"

Grace fumbled with a section of the lace from her apron for a moment and then dropped her head. "I…I suppose I was afraid."

"Of me?" Anne scoffed.

Grace nodded, continuing to fuss with her outfit. When next she spoke, her voice was but a whisper. "There are a great many things in this world to be afraid of."

Onyx sailed from above and landed at Grace's side, as if drawn by her retreat into sorrow. He carried a plump earthworm and laid it at her feet as if offering up his most coveted possession. She giggled and told him, "No, friend, that is yours." while fanning the writhing worm. "You go on ahead."

Lightness fell over Grace's features as her concentration returned. "I think we should not dwell on darkness on such a fine day. Let us bring more of this town to life!" She retrieved the journal from the spot where it had been abandoned during her fit and opened it. She leafed through the pages before settling upon one. "Here, read here," she directed, handing the journal to Anne.

July 4th, 1921

Our Independence celebration shall be held today and all the town is alive with excitement. Yesterday Mother and I helped Mrs. Roddenback bake dozens of tarts whilst Father and John joined in hanging decorations throughout town. –

A high, crackling noise grew in the foreground and both girls looked on as long garlands of red, white and blue paper materialized at the peaks of several houses. Seconds later, a long, wooden table erected before Mrs. Roddenback's house as if grown from the brush of an invisible painter. Star-capped pastries, lacquered with glaze, sprouted from its top like buds from the earth.

The girls locked eyes and then rose in tandem, bolting towards the spread. Grace arrived first and extinguished any hesitancy Anne might have labored with, cramming pastries into her mouth as fast as she was able.

"Boy, you must be hungry!" Anne exclaimed. She swiped two mini custard pies and quickly retracted, lest she lose a limb! "I 'spose you haven't had much to eat out here."

Grace flushed and lowered a half-eaten blueberry tart from her lips. While brushing crumbs from her face with the corner of her apron, she replied, "Just nuts and berries from the woods." She gazed longingly at the remaining pastries and added, "That is, until you kindly reopened the sweet shop."

"I take it you found a way in?" Anne couldn't suppress her grin.

Grace nodded, and a smile warmed her face. Anne mirrored her new friend, but turned cool when she spotted two pinpricks emerging near the head of town. Squinting into the distance, she asked Grace, "Do you see someone?"

Grace, who'd made nothing but purring noises for the last couple minutes, looked up from the last of Mrs. Roddenback's tarts as would a deer in hunter's sites. After following Anne's line of sight, she softly answered "Yes," and took a few steps back.

The figures grew closer, larger. Grace crinkled her brow as she gazed at them. "It's a boy, and a girl," she decided. As the pair passed under the New Year's banner, they swelled to the size of salt and peppershakers. A small groan leaked from Grace's lips before she told Anne, "The girl is Char." She stood on tiptoes and added, "And the boy, Josh."

"How'd you know who they are?"

Grace turned towards her, wearing a wicked smirk. "There isn't a great deal to do in a ghost town."

By the time the teens reached them, Anne and Grace had worn worry trails in the road. They were both familiar with Char's temper and neither girl was elated to see her charging forth. True to form, once Char came within earshot she was already rumbling. "Well, isn't this a cute lil' picnic!" she snarled. Josh, who trailed in her wake like a pack mule, kept quiet.

"Hi, Char." Anne forced a smile. "Hi, Josh."

"Hey." Josh peeped, maintaining his distance.

Char wore a knit crimson top that clashed with her hair. Somehow, both colors seemed angry, as though they were in fierce competition with one another. "Hey, baby girl. Who's your little friend?" she asked with an upturned nose.

"This is, um…this is Grace." Anne stumbled. She could feel Grace just behind her, quiet and still.

"Grace, huh?" Char snaked her head past Anne. "Looks more like a life-sized dolly to me." She came nearer, stopping shoulder to shoulder with Anne. "So…Grace," Char hissed. "You wouldn't happen to know anything about us getting locked out of our little treasure trove down there in the cellar, would you?"

Grace's dress brushed Anne's elbow as she shrank back. Char was so near now that her fruity shampoo fermented the air between them. Anne stepped backwards, positioning herself between the two girls and eye to eye with the red bull. "It was me, Char. I locked the cellar."

Char slowly twisted her head around, as would someone possessed by a demon. "Oh, it was you then?" she hissed. "I shoulda listened to Lexie." She crimped her lip until a fang showed through. "And here I thought you were smarter than that." She drew nearer, just inches from Anne's nose. Her breath was hot.

"Hey, Char, why don't you cool it?" Josh approached from the foreground, his white T-shirt fluttering like a peace flag.

"And why don't you mind your own business?"

Josh stumbled backwards, as though blown by an intense wind. Eyes downcast, he whispered, "Just sayin'," as he zipped up his jacket.

Anne's face sizzled as Char's focus returned there. "So, you know what's gonna happen now?" Char growled, "You're gonna march your little baby fanny down there and unlock it."

Another brush from Grace's dress tickled at Anne's elbow when she stepped forward and piped, "No, Charlotte. I think what must happen now is that you must leave and stop badgering my friend." A chill shot up Anne's arm as Grace linked hers beneath it. "I believe you've outworn your welcome here," Grace stiffly added.

Char inhaled deeply, swelling her chest an inch. Steam seemed to spew from her ears as she snarled, "Oh, I have, have I?" Her nostrils flared and as the sunlight passed through them, they turned electric pink. "And just what are you gonna do, if I don't?"

Grace took a deep breath of her own and lifted her head high. "Well, then, I suppose I shall have to speak with your friend Brittany about the little interlude between her beau and yourself that took place here just a night ago."

Char's face froze and then fell as if thawed by her own fire. Retreating to Josh's elbow, she whimpered like a wounded animal, "Let's get outta here." A few feet away she made a snide addition about not caring to "play with babies" but never looked back.

Once the teens had shrunk to the size of chess pieces on the horizon, Anne slid from Grace's grip and locked eyes with her. "Thank you. Thanks for bailing me out. No one's ever really done anything like that for me before."

"I was pleased to," Grace returned. "You're my friend, after all. And as it would seem, the only one I have in the world, at present." She smiled coyly, as Anne returned her affectionate expression, but startled when a chime broke through the air between them.

Onyx erupted into a flapping fit on Mrs. Roddenback's porch rail while Grace made a similar display, shuttering her ears and yowling. "What in God's name was that?"

"Oh, sorry." Anne silenced the alarm on her watch. "I've gotta go."

Grace glanced at the sun sinking in the sky. "But the hour is not so late."

"Yeah, I know. It's just that I was out here super-late yesterday and I promised my aunt I'd go on errands with her today. She and my uncle sorta wig out if I don't show up when I said I would." Watching Grace, Anne noted a despondent look. "Hey, why don't you come with me?"

"Oh, oh, I…" Grace stumbled. "No, I don't think that wise." She focused in the distance and her eyes sparked. "But perhaps there is something you might do for me before you go?"

After a quick jaunt to the tart table, Grace returned with her journal in hand. Thumbing through the pages while muttering to herself, she settled on one and held the dairy out to Anne. "Read this for me?"

"Sure thing." Anne took the book and her expression lit up. "Hey, so do you think I have magic powers or something?" Images of wands, cloaks and cackling villains swelled in her mind.

Grace shrugged and popped her eyebrows. "Perhaps. Or perhaps the book's been bewitched by its long stay in the trunk." Before Anne had a mind to inquire further, Grace had snatched the diary back. "Here, why don't I try?" she excitedly suggested, speeding towards the head of town with her black curls bouncing in rhythm with her strides. "Come on!"

Streaking against the backdrop of her ancient house, Grace was a picture from a bygone era. She raced up its bowing steps, as would a child to Christmas morning, and charged through the "Door to Nowhere" without so much as a second glance.

Anne trailed behind with much more cautious steps. The light inside the house was faint and, as she entered, Anne skirted the edge of the foyer's walls, half expecting the gaping hole she'd created weeks earlier to open like the mouth of a grave and swallow her whole. The musk of fresh-cut wood still hung in the air. In the darkness she found the freshly cut boards lighting her way.

"Come on!" Grace's cream tights flashed across the catwalk on the second floor, slowing only slightly as she passed the portion of missing railing where Anne had fallen. Anne ascended the stairs, and slunk behind her friend like a tightrope walker. The drop looked even more intimidating now that she'd experienced it.

A long, narrow hallway branched from the precarious walkway and Anne felt her muscles unclench as she set foot there. She followed it to the room at its conclusion and found Grace sitting cross-legged on the floor, surrounded by a rusted metal bed frame and peeling wallpaper. The journal sat open in her lap, and as Anne entered, Grace motioned her over. "Come, sit with me. I'll read to you."

August 24th, 1921

For the first time, dear diary, I write to you from the comfort of my very own room! Father made a production of it, wrapping me in a blindfold and leading me down the hallway until we reached my door. My very own door! When he took the cover away, I was without words. He and Mother have made me such a beautiful sanctuary! I was crafted a new bed by Charles Vickor, the ironsmith, and Mother sewed a lovely lilac quilt with which to top it. It must be the softest thing I have ever felt!

Father special-ordered matching violet wallpaper all the way from Seattle and papered the entire room last week. It is the same shade of purple as the violets that grow in the valley each spring. Lovely!

I am in heaven. Surely I will rest well tonight!

Queen for a day,

Grace Rowden

Anne watched the walls with anticipation, but the grey strips of wallpaper still hung there like wilting petals. The bed, still corroded and bowing, lay unchanged. Grace's face fell.

"Hmph. Maybe it was me. Maybe I am magic." Anne swallowed a peal of delight.

"Wait, look!"

Beneath their feet, the worn floorboards warmed from grey to amber. Life seemed to climb the walls as the peels of wallpaper ironed themselves and lay flat. Pale-yellow water rings and dingy grey melted away, leaving bright violet behind. A creak of bending metal pealed through the room as the bed bent and stretched to find its original form. Once revitalized, a downy purple quilt appeared at its foot and rolled up the length as if drawn by invisible hands.

"Holy crap!" Anne exclaimed, admiring the room with excited senses.

Grace sprung to her feet and leapt onto the bed, rolling across it and back again, like a dog would in something foul.

Burying her face in the quilt, she breathed in deep, and then exhaled satisfaction. She was positively glowing. Moments later, as she bid Anne farewell and waved from beneath the New Year's banner, she still radiated brightly enough to defy the darkness encroaching all around her.

Chapter Six

"I don't want to hear it. Not one more cockamamie excuse!" Claudia was eclipsing the front doorway as Anne approached. Her eyes burned bright, warning the hour, as they ignited the night sky outside. "From the sounds of it, you've been cookin' up alotta those lately. Even found out about your little vandalism spree!"

Anne looked sideways and up, anywhere but at her aunt's face. "Vandalism spree?"

"Don't play dumb with me, missy!" Claudia had foam rollers in her hair that rattled like Medusa's snakes as she railed. "And here I thought we had some hooligans runnin' around here, messin' with Lexie's bikes. Come to find out it was you all along!"

Lexie's head appeared atop her mother's shoulder, perched as a bird would. She puckered and kissed the air before vanishing with a parting cackle. Clearly, Char had told her of the transgression in Devlin earlier that day.

"Well, don't just stand there! Get your butt inside. Storm's comin'," Claudia commanded while scowling.

Anne did as she was told, stealing a glance at the sky as it passed overhead. Thick, ashen clouds pregnant with rain loomed above. Encroaching from the west, a mass of blackened-blue warned of heavy rain to come.

Claudia flattened against the open door to allow her niece passage inside. Squeezing through the sliver-sized opening, Anne imagined herself a career criminal returning to prison after failing at a life in normal society. Once in the house, she kept her head down and asked after the storm.

"Kinda snuck up on us," Claudia admitted, maintaining a cross tone. "Gonna be a doozy though. Flood and high-wind warnings all through the valley." She nodded towards the front door, just as they rounded the corner into the kitchen. "Pat's out there battin' down the hatches right now."

Minutes later, wind whistled from the entryway, announcing Pat's return. Dressed in a hooded, brown rain suit with only his soggy beard peeking out, he was the most convincing Sasquatch Anne had ever seen. "Man alive, it's nasty out there!" he exclaimed. He kicked his hood back, and an avalanche of raindrops fell to the floor.

"Dammit, Pat!" Claudia was holding onto her irritation as if it were a sack full of dollar bills.

Pat muttered "Sorry," and then shuffled to the laundry room, leaving a shiny, slug-like trail in his wake.

Claudia only rumbled and then waddled towards the oven door. A tang of tomato sauce seasoned the air as she pulled it open to reveal a tray of manicotti inside. Aside from a few decades-old tarts,

Anne hadn't eaten all day, and as she breathed in, her mouth watered.

"Oh, no, you don't," Claudia growled, watching her niece. "This ain't a meal for vandals and liars." She turned her back, made a few selections from the pantry and in two minutes flat produced a stale peanut-butter-and-jelly sandwich and a satisfied smile. "Why don't you just take this on down to Lexie's room to eat? You can stew in there a while…Think about all the crap you've been pullin' lately."

"Yes, ma'am." Anne accepted her plate, while still leering at the manicotti, and sulked down the hall. Alone in Lexie's still room, she abandoned her sandwich on the dresser, collapsed on her under-filled air mattress and listened to the rain. It came in swells, pummeling the roof so hard that Anne feared it might break through. She imagined the wind stripping the house, layer by layer, until it had forced its way inside and engulfed them all in a cold, miserable deluge. And in an instant, she was back in Devlin. She saw the threadbare house of her nightmares copied, over and over again, along its streets. She saw peeling walls and crumbling bricks. She saw a wailing monsoon ravaging the fragile remains of half-decayed roofs and rotted porches. Right in the middle of it all, she saw Grace. "Oh, my God, she's gonna drown!"

Before Anne had the time and good sense to second-guess her actions, she was saddling the window jam in Lexie's bedroom. It was a short drop to the ground, but by the time she'd found her feet and snuck a bicycle from the shed beside the garage, Anne's clothes were already soaked through. Raindrops pelted her like bullets as she rode. They came so fast and so hard that only the white fog lines on either side of the road kept her from unwittingly riding into a ditch. When she finally reached the forest, its thick canopy opened like an umbrella over her. Inside, the squall was weakened as it passed through layers of trees boughs. Its howls echoed from every direction, as if enraged by its failure to break through.

Over the crest and free of the trees, the wind revived and gnashed at Anne's body more angrily than ever. Shielding her face, she coasted the length of the decline and sailed beneath what remained of the New Year's banner, before uncovering her eyes. Though the fierce wind blurred her vision, Anne could see clearly enough to be stupefied by the sight that lay before her. Immediately to her right, a powder pink house glowed with fresh paint. It had been stripped of ivy, and where a heap of rotted wood had once stood, now sat instead a dazzling ivory porch. The windows, once riddled with holes and filth, sparkled in the night, reflecting the rain as it fell.

A few houses down, another of the Victorian charmers stood bright against the inky torrent. Dressed in luminous white, it blazed like a lighthouse in the storm. Orange light spilled from its front windows, and as Anne passed and looked inside, she marveled at a set of button-tufted couches and an ornate coffee table, still shining with fresh polish. The hearth glowed with fire, and directly in front of it sat Grace, warming her hands.

"Hey!" Anne erupted. She pressed her face to one of the windowpanes and rapped alongside it. The breeze bellowed behind her, its voice far louder. "Hey! Grace!" This time she pounded, and Grace immediately stiffened, her head jerking left, then right. Fright riddled her features.

"Here! I'm right here!" Anne balled her fist and gave the window a wallop that finally drew Grace's attention and brought her to the front door.

"My goodness, you look like a drowned rat!" Grace greeted her. She flailed like a wisp in the doorway, blown sideways as the wind entered alongside her friend. "What in God's name are you doing out in this?!"

Anne staggered in, nearly toppling over as a gust kicked at her hind side. "Well, I was looking for you," she sputtered, still catching her breath. "I was worried about you drowning in one of these wonky old houses." Steadying herself on a nearby banister, Anne panned the room, and added, "But it looks like you're pretty darn comfy!"

Grace trotted past her, lifted the journal from a stone slab beneath the fireplace, and then galloped back. "You wouldn't believe all of the amazing things, Anne! You wouldn't believe all of the things I've brought to life!" Her eyes gleamed as she clutched the book to her chest.

"Really?"

"Really and truly!" she exclaimed, returning to the hearth. Grace cradled the book and then made a sideways glance under the coffee table. "Isn't that right, Onyx?"

A caw leaked from beneath the table, and Anne stooped to the sight of a partially saturated raven wrapped in a frilly, pink receiving blanket. "It was all I could read out," Grace admitted, stifling a giggle. She petted the diary and then drummed the floor beside her. "Come. Read with me."

"I can't." Anne wrung a section of her hair, and an unseemly amount of water dribbled out. "I'm in pretty deep with my aunt and uncle. Plus, I sorta left without telling them." Her shoes squished as she shifted her weight and she grimaced. "They're probably gonna lock me up for the rest of the summer, as it is," she moaned.

The jovial quality in Grace's voice evaporated as she replied, "Oh, no. Oh, dear." Wrinkles sprouted in the middle of her forehead. "And that's all my doing, isn't it? You came all this way in this horrid storm and risked your freedom, all to ensure my welfare."

"It's not your fault. It was my choice," Anne said, forcing a smile. She turned to leave but paused as Grace's footsteps pounded the floorboards just behind her.

"Perhaps, if I could explain? Perhaps, then, they would understand?" Grace asked, circling around to face her.

"Naw, they're not that kind of people," Anne confessed, continuing towards the door. "And, anyway, what would we say? That you're my hundred-year-old friend who I brought to life by reading a diary?" Out loud it sounded even more bizarre than she'd imagined.

"But…but I don't think I can bear it. I can't bear it if I'm here all alone," Grace blubbered. "What if I never see you again? What if I go mad, with only this raven to talk to?"

Anne reached out to steady Grace's trembling hands. "Then come with me! Come with me back to the house. There's food, and it's warm, and we'll be together," she encouraged.

Grace crumpled her chin and her eyes grew hollow. Her hands felt limp in Anne's. "Oh, no. No, I couldn't do that. I couldn't stay there," she squeaked.

"Why not? Why can't you? You can't stay here forever." Anne tightened her grip, lending a squeeze of reassurance. "Look, how 'bout this…you come with me and you can make up your mind, when you get there, if you want to stay. We'll just think up something to tell my aunt and uncle on the way. I've been getting pretty good at coming up with excuses lately." She cracked a smile and felt Grace's hands warm in hers.

"Very well," Grace conceded, following close behind as Anne resumed her path towards the front door.

Outside, the storm was fading, but cursing with its last breaths. Onyx took to flight, fading into one of the few dark clouds that remained like sputters from a dying engine. The girls trailed underneath, Grace pointing out the houses she'd awakened while Anne was away. There were five in total, all that had a place in the diary's pages. As she left them behind, Grace blew each one a farewell kiss, and promised, "Mommy will return very soon."

The forest lay in shambles, like the aftermath of children run amok on Halloween. Fallen leaves littered the ground like empty candy wrappers. "Watch out for that limb. Kinda sneaks up on you," Anne warned, navigating around yet another downed tree branch, as she strained against the dark. "And there's one up there, too, on the right."

"Thanks." Grace gathered her skirt and stepped cautiously, shivering as a gust of wind shot up her thigh.

The sound of snapping twigs filled the night air as the girls labored forth in the blackness. Anne struggled to gather her bearings, until she caught a sliver of light in the near distance. "I think we're about there. I think I can see the clearing up ahead," she announced. Somehow, the bare clay ground outside the forest illuminated the night, calling to them like a beacon. Anne stepped over the ring and sat down on the other side with a sigh of relief. Following behind her, Grace made a low groan, as if straining to lift a very heavy object.

"I…I can't get over it," Grace called out, following a grunt. "I just…I keep trying to move forward, but it's as if something is holding me back." Grace's left foot was hovering just above the ring, her torso tilted forward as though she were leaning face-first into a wall.

Anne dashed towards the boulders, a taste of déjà vu ringing on her tongue. "Oh, oh…I know what to do!" She canvassed Grace's body and found the journal poking from her apron front pocket. "Just drop the journal. You just have to put it in the bushes or something. You can't leave Devlin with it."

Grace placed her left foot back on enchanted ground and her face went ghostly white. "What did you just say?"

"I said you have to ditch the journal. You can't leave Devlin if you have it." Anne chuckled and curled her lip. "Trust me, I know."

"Where did you hear that awful name?"

"What name?" Anne inched forward until her toes grazed a boulder shining with a fresh coat of rain. "Devlin?"

Grace nodded, her mouth downturned.

"An old guy at the library. He told me that was the town's name."

In the silent space between them, Onyx's arrival announced itself with a flap no louder than a whisper. He landed at Grace's feet with a light crumpling of leaves, sauntered over and began rubbing against her leg, as would a cat. She gazed at him affectionately and then glowered at Anne. "Well, it's not. That's a filthy, nasty name that those people in the city crafted."

"Oh, okay. Sorry," Anne sputtered, feeling badly without knowing exactly why. "So what is the name?"

Grace's words were cool as she replied. "It has none. It was not ours to name." Her long black hair hung across her face, partially obscuring a look of dread. "It has belonged to the Faerie, always."

Anne fell silent, struggling for a reply. In the stillness, a clap of thunder echoed overhead, announcing a wall of storm clouds as they approached from the west. After a glance skyward, Anne warned, "Look, we can talk about all that later. For now, we've gotta go." She pointed up, adding, "I think round two is coming."

"Yes, alright," Grace replied. She stowed the journal in the same leafy bed Anne had made for it weeks ago and then returned to the ring's edge. Yet as she moved to cross it, she met the same invisible barrier a second time. She raised her arms and clapped her hands flat upon it, as would a mime. "They won't...they won't let me go," she stammered, her eyes welling up. "I knew it. I knew I'd never get away. I knew when Father locked me in that awful trunk that I'd be a prisoner for all my days." She was shaking now, flailing against the invisible bars that held her captive.

Anne reached out and grabbed hold of Grace's right arm, but as much as she pulled, she could not draw it beyond the ring. "I don't understand. This should work!" she exclaimed. Grace's distress was infectious, and Anne felt her own voice vibrating as it crept up her throat a second time. "Who is it? Who won't let you leave?" She began glancing madly about the forest rim, searching for some ominous figure hidden in the shadows.

"The Faerie! The offering! I was chosen!" Grace howled. Anne had hold of both her arms now, but they refused to move, as though fixed in concrete. "You read the journal. You must know! I am theirs! Father hid me away, but you see what good it's done. For his betrayal, they took everyone, and they'll not rest until they have me, too!"

Anne released Grace's arms, and the force of their parting sent both girls tumbling backwards on their respective sides of the Faerie ring. Onyx squawked as Grace hit the ground, nearly landing on him. "Wait…what?" Anne sputtered. "That's where everyone went? That was the big disappearance all those years ago? You think a bunch of little faeries took everyone in town?"

"There is no thinking about it. That's precisely what occurred." Grace stood and brushed off her backside, scowling. "I saw you read it: my entry about Tobias. I know you know. The bounty, the prosper of the town…it was all the magic of the Faerie. They allowed us to dwell here, but in exchange they took a child into the realm each season and transformed him into a Changeling by assuming his body." Grace stomped off and returned with the journal. Pointing it at Anne like a weapon, she resembled a soldier forced to make his first kill. "It was I! I who was chosen that final season! I who condemned all of my friends and my family with my cowardice! And it is I who shall live for all eternity with the weight of their aimless souls upon me!"

Anne scratched her head and simultaneously donned conflicting expressions of both empathy and doubt, which married on her face to form an altogether peculiar-looking mask. "We're talkin' faeries here, right…like Tinkerbell? Little shiny wings and pixie dust?"

"Oh, how you've been fooled, my friend," Grace rumbled.

"That's the façade they'd like you to see! Images of those doe-eyes vixens have been passed down through the ages, all in an attempt to lure you in. Make no mistake, the Fae are evil-spirited little demons with dark hearts that no amount of Faerie glamour can hide."

Anne's legs weakened beneath her. She could hear her heart-beat quickening. "So, what? These creepy little things wore the kids in your town like human suits?"

Grace made a sharp nod, and said, "That's a Changeling," in a hollow voice.

"But…but why would you feel to blame? I thought you said it was your father who hid you? In the trunk, right?"

"Yes, but that's of little matter," Grace replied, not looking up. She was pacing now, wearing a path through the leaves. Onyx hopped behind her like an obedient poodle. The more the seconds ticked by, the faster her gait became. There was anger in her steps, and as they pounded the earth, it was growing. "This weight…this incessant guilt and loneliness, it's unbearable! Trapped not in their world, not in yours…just stuck here in Purgatory. At least before, in the nothingness, there was peace." She glared at the journal still in her hand, fire welling in her eyes. "I wish I'd never written this godforsaken thing!" she exclaimed, tossing the book several yards away. Both girls looked on as it fell to the earth. The wind blew it open, causing its pages to flap madly, like the wings of a bird trying desperately to take flight.

Even stifled by the whistling wind, the sharp breath drawn by Grace was electric. "Oh, my: how could I have missed it? Perhaps there is a way! Perhaps I can fix it all!" She stood still for a moment and then took off at a sprint towards the diary.

"What? What is it?" Anne followed along from the opposite side of the ring. Epiphany struck like a hot iron as she loped. "Are you thinking of reading them out? Could we read out your friends and family?"

Scooping it into her arms, Grace fondled the book as would a child her only doll. "Oh, no. I'm afraid not. I had hoped so, at one time, but they'd have appeared alongside me long ago. You've read of them all too often."

Anne came to a standstill and scratched at her head. "Oh. I wonder why?" she asked.

"I don't believe they exist here anymore in this forgotten town, where all time seems to have stopped." Grace's shoulders bowed and her tone grew wistful. "When they did not come alive as you read of them, that's when I knew. I knew they'd been taken by the Faerie…into their realm."

"Oh," Anne breathed, falling quiet.

The rain was returning, and droplets pinged in the background as they glanced off bushes along the ring's edge. The storm was not done with them yet. Anne watched pensively as the drops grew in size and number. Grounded again, she returned her attentions to

Grace. "Okay, so I don't get it then. What can we do, then? How can we fix it?"

"Well, that all depends," Grace began, leafing through the journal's damp pages. She narrowed her eyes on the book and backed up until sheltered under the canopy of a nearby tree. With her concentration fixed, she was quiet for several minutes before asking Anne, "How are you at battling demons?"

Chapter Seven

Anne went numb. Raindrops pelted her backside, growing in number and fury as she dismissed them.

"If I can't undo what has been done, I will do what must be," Grace proclaimed, stowing the journal beneath her apron bib. She studied Anne through saturated locks of hair that hung like vines over her eyes. Despite their strain, her features were resolute. "I must go back for them, with or without you, my friend."

The word "friend" resonated in Anne's ears, and she looked back at the only one she'd known in a very long while. "Well…" she began with a tremor, "I'm not totally sure what I'm signing up for. But since Claudia'll surely kill me once I get back, anyway, I might as well give someone else a go first!"

Grace's brilliant smile illuminated the darkness. "Splendid!" She made a small clap that sloshed between her wet hands. "You shall see. All will come clear with the sunrise."

* * *

Following a restless night huddled together at the foot of a dying hearth, Grace led Anne to the edge of the wood beyond the town's borders. There, the trees became increasingly bare and the foliage turned from green to a dull brown. An odious rot spoiled the air. "It's just up here, up ahead," Grace announced in a quivering tone. "You'll see it soon."

When the Mound came into view, it required no introduction. It was massive: a monstrous heap of earth erupting like a boil from the flat ground. From a distance, Anne detected movement atop it, and as they came nearer, she saw that the slender trees dotting the hill were undulating. Watching as she gaped at them, Grace whispered, "They say they shriek—the trees. They shriek when they're cut. The people in town said their cries would wake the Faerie." Grace's gaze lingered in their shared silence. Her voice was almost too quiet to hear as she mused, "I wonder how Father managed to cut one without them knowing."

Hypnotized by the swaying branches, Anne did not look away as she responded, "Oh, yeah — for your trunk. Man, that thing was creepy. I dunno how you could stand having it around."

"I had no choice," Grace breathed. "Its magic is what shielded me. Without it, the Faerie surely would've discovered my hiding place." She exhaled and dipped her head. "But perhaps that would've been for the best."

Anne stepped near her friend and placed a hand on Grace's shoulder. "No, don't say that. After all, we're gonna fix it, right?"

"Right!" Grace pulled the journal from the crook of her arm and parted the pages to one that she'd dog-eared. Its date read

March 20, 1921.

"Hey, that looks familiar. Isn't that—?"

"Yes, 'tis. The very page that drew me to you."

Still peering over Grace's shoulder, Anne stammered, "But… but I thought you said not to read that."

At no more than a whisper, Grace replied, "Yes, I know," and began tracing her fingertip over the incantation written there. "I feared that in reading it, you'd bring the portal to life—that you'd bring forth the Faerie."

Anne's pulse doubled, and she shrank backwards, catching her heel on a rock and narrowly avoiding a tumble. By the time she regained her footing, she was several yards away. Projecting her voice only amplified its alarm, as she asked, "And now?"

"Now I believe that it's the only way to save my friends and family," Grace replied, not looking at her. "It is because of me that they're trapped. And if I am not the one to save them, then whom?"

Grace's question met only silence as Anne struggled to refute her friend's logic. They both gawked at the Mound in a shared stupor until a flash of motion from the sky announced Onyx's arrival. He sailed effortlessly downwards and landed near Grace's feet with a thud. "Hello, friend," she greeted him, before the bird took flight a second time and then landed on her shoulder, causing her left side to dip. Grace nuzzled him and then paused again in quiet reflection, this time scrutinizing the book in her hands. After a short while, she turned to Anne and announced, "I think you should stay."

Anne's legs had been married to the ground since she'd stumbled, but they began pulsating beneath her, as if awakened from an extended sleep. "Oh, no, you don't," she barked while marching towards Grace and her tar-feathered parrot. "I'm not letting you go in there alone. Besides," she teased, glancing at Onyx, "every pirate knows you can't go out pillaging without your trusty crewmate!"

"Quite true." Grace's cheeks plumped as she drew a smile. "You are a good friend."

"Yeah, I am," Anne replied with a wink. "So should you read, or should I?"

Grace shrugged.

"What do you think will happen?"

"I'm not sure," Grace confessed while still looking at the book. "I've seen the portal opened before and a Faerie was always there waiting. But as they are not expecting us, perhaps we'll find ourselves alone?" Her doubtful expression was anything but reassuring.

Anne scanned the ground around them, stopping as she passed over a fallen tree limb shaped like a baton. She picked it up and gripped it as though she were about to bat for the Yankees. "Well then, let's get it over with."

With a nod of encouragement, Grace began.

Folk of the Wood

Who have given us prosper

We call to you now

With our child to offer

Come ye now forth

Faerie chosen to morph

And enter our fold

As to human you mold.

As the final word of the incantation left Grace's lips, the trees atop the Mound froze. Stick-straight arrows to the heavens, not even their wilted leaves fluttered with the movement of the wind. The girls stiffened, along with the trunks, until a groaning began deep down inside the Mound. The sound grew steadily louder and nearer the surface as if a monstrous child was inside, burrowing out of its mother's womb. Near its zenith, a small hole appeared at the Mound's base. It was tiny at first, perhaps the size of a marble, but widened rapidly, dirt spilling backwards through it like sand running from an hourglass. In seconds, a peach could've passed through. Another few seconds, and a basketball would've fit. At the close of a full minute, it provided a perfectly round doorway big enough for a human child to enter.

A green shroud sprouted over the opening and Anne found herself scanning it for an ominous figure as horrific as any she could imagine. "Are, they...err...is it...usually standing there?"

Grace only nodded and crept forward on tiptoes, Onyx rocking on her shoulder as he attempted to center his weight. His claws dug into her dress, but she didn't seem to notice.

Anne trailed behind, gripping her bat with eyes still trained on the sheath of moss that covered the portal entrance. The moss was sticky and as they pushed through it held them back like the grotesque fingers of a wicked witch. It scratched at Anne's throat and tugged at her hair until she winced aloud.

"Shhhh." Grace put a finger to her lips and parted the final swath of the curtain, holding it aside for her friend to step through.

Beyond the green lay a blanket of deadness. The ground, the trees and even the sky were all some varied shade of grey, as though sucked dry of color. A long path lay ahead, twisting through bleak rows of leafless trees and half-rotted shrubbery. The earth was flat and the horizon went on forever, filled with endless acres of the same image duplicated over and over again. In the far distance, Anne spied large, dark masses in several of the trees, but they only added to the overall bleakness of the place. The half-risen sun, with its dull charcoal haze, resembled the cooked yolk of a rotten egg sliding from the sky. "Holy cow, this place is a dive," Anne declared. "Boy, did Disney have it wrong."

Grace raised one eyebrow and gazed at the unending skyline.

"I mean, I thought these guys were supposed to be all bountiful and prosperous and whatnot. This place looks like a desert, or something." Anne breathed in. Even the air was stale.

"Oh. No. It doesn't work quite that way. The Faerie magic works differently in our world than theirs. Father said that's part of why they covet our existence. They long for our comforts, our faculties. That is why they prize the Changeling gift as they do. They envy so. It drives them mad." Grace was cautiously scanning as she spoke, though the ground surrounding them was so barren that any creature would've been visible for miles.

"Humph." Anne studied the wasteland and felt a weight building in her chest. "I guess that explains why the forest got so ruddy looking the closer we got to this place."

"Oh, yes, it's infected," Grace agreed, adding a nod. Onyx leapt from her shoulder, crunching on the dry earth as he landed there. It was the only sound they'd heard since arriving.

"It's so quiet."

"'Tis," Grace agreed at a hush. She brushed back her long hair, straightened her apron, and drew a breath. "So, shall we?"

"If we have to."

They set out upon the dusty road that stretched before them, canvassing the trees as they walked. A short distance in, Anne's lungs stung as though all their moisture had been sucked away. Her lips grew tender, the skin hardened. It seemed they walked for miles, and yet the images before them remained unchanged. Even the ashen sun slipping into the earth remained fixed in its spot on the horizon. "I don't feel like we're getting anywhere," Anne confessed. Her throat itched as she spoke.

"I'd been thinking the very same thing." Grace stopped and a cloud of dust puffed beneath her feet. "Perhaps if we enter the wood?"

"I guess it couldn't hurt," Anne decided. She diverted from the path and approached the bank of alders that lined it. As she snaked through two bare trees with bark like the skin of Saharan lizards, disorientation swelled in her gut. The sensation of passing through dozens of doors in the breadth of one step rocked her body.

Close at her heels, Grace heaved, "Oh, my Lord!" just as a nest of vegetation sprouted before them. Suddenly their surroundings were completely different, as though they'd been transported from one end of the world to the other. More muddied than the preceding terrain, this land was thick with rotting brush, as if several layers of dead forest had been laid atop one another, until they all combined into one mucky mess. When Anne was a child, her mother had often read to her from a pop-up Grimm's fairytale book. At the close of the book, all of the pages piled over one another and created a haunting image of a deep, dark forest. Anne had since seen it many times in her nightmares, but this was the first time the image had appeared to her waking eyes.

"I think I preferred the barren wastelands back there," Anne half-joked, gawking at trees with their heads full of decayed leaves.

The flora was so dense that she could not see more than a few feet in front of her. It was terribly cold, as if wetness had saturated the very bones of the earth. Rot hung in the air. Anne pulled her jacket tight and buried her hands in her pockets.

With Onyx leading the way from above, the girls began thrashing their way through the brush. There was no path to speak of, and just a short ways in, Grace had already torn her fine dress to ribbons on the thorny scrub. Drops of crimson trickled down her milky legs as she assured, "I'm fine, just fine."

They'd hiked for nearly an hour, making slow progress, before Anne mustered the courage to ask, "So, what exactly are we looking for?" Her body immediately tensed to a state of ready, as though her question may bring about an assault from the shadows.

Grace, still shadowing her friend's footsteps, squeaked, "Anything I suppose," just as a slight rustle warned ahead. Both girls came to a halt and stared into the distance, where a flutter caught Anne's eye. Her focus increased, along with the tension, as the flicker repeated.

"Ah, it's only Onyx!" Anne announced, following a sigh of relief. The bird's glossy feathers contrasted their dull surroundings, like a piece of the wrong puzzle mixed in with the rest. Anne's heartbeat steadied as she stepped over a mangle of shrubs to approach him. "Hey, birdie. Where you been?"

Onyx dipped his head and bobbed back up again as if to greet them. Smiling back at him, Anne moved to sidestep the tree on which he'd perched, but she was cut short as Onyx leapt from his gnarled branch and landed directly in her path. "Hey, you goofy bird, what are you playing at?" She dodged to the right and was once again blocked by a quick interception from the raven. Anne pursed her lips, with the intent to berate him, but felt suddenly still, all color draining from her face. "Did you hear that?" she asked Grace at a hush.

Grace moved close, dropping her tone to match. "Hear what?"

The sound was more distinct as Anne heard it a second time: muffled scratching. It seemed to emanate from a bushy knoll, a hundred or so yards ahead. "That. That noise. You hear it?"

The girls locked eyes and Grace silently nodded just as Onyx stepped clear of the path. All three crept forward with palpable caution, as though one misstep may send them plummeting to the bowels of Hell. Quiet as the dead, they drew nearer to its source, and as they did, the scraping became more pronounced. Within in a few yards, other odd noises joined the fray and their peculiar melody was disquieting.

A massive, withered tree lay at the crest of the knoll, and as they approached it, the clatter amplified even further. They approached at a crawl, and scaled the small hill on hands and knees. As Grace made the climb, any light left on her snowy, white dress vanished forever.

At the top of the rise, the tree's massive roots ran along the length of the ridge like a wall. Anne and Grace gripped the edge of the largest of them and peered over top to find a shallow valley, where two creatures stirred. The beasts' backs were turned, and with bodies nearly identical in color to their forest surroundings, their features were difficult to distinguish. They were huddled around a makeshift pit, and they held long, slender hands over it, as if warming them by a fire, though none burned there. Both were crouching and alternated between miming enjoyment of the imaginary heat and balancing on the ground, as would apes. Their bodies were long and thin, with rib bones exposed beneath taut, dirty flesh. Almost entirely naked, only bits of bark and dead moss covered their privates.

One of the creatures rose and retrieved a makeshift pot from beside a nearby log. It was made of bark with a bony twig for a handle. Returning to the fire pit, he hung it from a bent branch that ran overhead, rattling a ladle that sat inside. Next, he gripped the ladle and gestured as if pouring soup into small bark-clad cups that the second creature held out.

"What are they doing?" Anne quietly asked.

Grace gave only a blank expression in reply and then returned to observing the scene in the valley below, where the first of the beings had accepted the cup and kicked his head back as if drinking from it. As he lowered the mug, his head ticked in the direction of their hiding spot, and Anne shuddered. The creature's eyes were black as ink and without pupils, without a soul. His hollow face was as ashen as the barren main road on which they'd arrived. However, neither of these repugnant features disturbed Anne nearly as much as his lack of a mouth. Just below his nose sat a blank space with only a puckered little knot, no bigger than a bellybutton, where a mouth ought to have been. Anne gasped.

The sprite's inkwell eyes panned towards the root behind which the girls were hidden, seemingly drawn by Anne's small gasp. "Oh, my, I think they've heard us," Grace's whisper quivered. "Come on," she urged, tugging at Anne's pant leg. Grace inched backwards on hands and knees, stopping after just a couple short feet.

"What's wrong?" Anne asked, still focused on the scene in the valley, where the second creature, a near doppelganger of the first, had now joined his companion in examining the ridge.

"I'm...I'm stuck." Grace's words came faster and louder than before. "Look!" she erupted, pointing at her ankle.

Anne followed Grace's line of sight and found a bright green vine coiled around the leg of her friend. Both girls looked on in disbelief as it began to grow before their very eyes, engulfing Grace's knee and spiraling up her thigh. Large, teardrop buds sprouted from its length, fattening as the stalk did.

Anne shimmied down the hill and joined Onyx, who'd begun pecking at the vine. Tender as it appeared, the plant was extremely tough, and despite Anne's repeated attempts to tear it away, no amount of force seemed sufficient to free Grace's leg. "Hurry! You must hurry!" Grace's voice was frantic. She raked at the vine and her whole body quaked. She could hear the Faerie nearing, just as Anne could.

"I'm trying! It's not working! It won't let go!" Abandoning her attempts to pull the vine away with her bare hands, Anne scanned the forest floor, searching for anything that might cut it, but such a carpet of rot lie there that little more was visible than mud and decayed vegetation. "It's—it's so thick. I can't tear it off!"

In the space of a breath, Grace became very still. Her harrowed eyes married with Anne's. "Leave, Anne. You must leave me."

"I won't."

"You must." Grace's manner was grave, but it grew more so as leaves crackled just feet away.

Anne sputtered, "I...I..." but was cut short by an alarming squawk from Onyx, who bolted as a second rustle erupted from a semi-circle of trees just behind them. There, the intertwined branches of two large oaks parted to reveal an old man standing between them. He was thin and filthy, with a mop of snowy white hair. He wore coverings of the wood, and his gaunt face resembled a skeleton mask that Anne had worn three Halloweens ago. Supported on a cane fashioned from a gnarled stick, he hobbled towards them without a word. In his free hand, he carried a hatchet of sorts, made of a slice of flint affixed to a log handle with twine. Labored by age, he slowly drew the axe high and leveled it over the girls. Anne had only time enough to wail, "No!", and throw herself over the top of Grace before the axe came down, slicing the green tether in two.

"Come here. Follow me," the old man directed, retreating to the trees without looking back.

The girls locked eyes, their silence amplifying the menacing sounds mounting just over the ridge. They intertwined their hands and copied his footsteps, disappearing into the thicket just as a set of bony fingers gripped the root beneath which they'd previously hidden.

A tunnel made of woven branches lay beyond the oaks, and handicapped as the old man was, it was all the girls could do to keep pace with their guide. Onyx sailed overhead, his wing tips brushing the sides of the tunnel as he went. Several yards in, the ceiling dipped, and the raven, no longer able to fly, descended and landed upon the old man's shoulder.

"What's up with that?" Anne puffed. She was near breathless and when Grace failed to reply, she was thankful for the excuse to stop and rest. She turned to face the path behind her and found Grace still a hundred feet back, dragging her leg as if it were broken. "Oh, my gosh, are you alright?" Anne asked, rushing to her side.

"Yes, I think so. It feels like it's gone to sleep." Beads of sweat glistened on Grace's forehead. Her face had gone pale.

"Here, let me help," Anne offered. She slung Grace's right arm over her own shoulder, and with their efforts combined, they regained sight of their mysterious escort in a matter of minutes. His head of white hair bobbed like a giant lure in the faint light, Onyx's silhouette still rocking against it.

Up ahead, the tunnel broke and split in two. Their white rabbit vanished down the left hole and so the girls followed in kind, still alert for any footsteps that might follow behind them. A few more twists and turns through various offshoots, and then a dim light emerged ahead. Nearing it, Anne felt certain that the illumination was created by sunlight, but as they passed through and into the open space beyond, it was an odd sort of moonlight that fell upon them. Looking skyward, Grace hissed, "My stars, it's hideous."

Directly overhead, an orb of black shone, casting a metallic haze on the forest that lay beneath. Anne gaped at the trees, the foliage and the earth, all of them a varied degree of nightshade. She felt suddenly blind and fumbled to find her footing in the mire. With one arm still supporting Grace, Anne extended the other and fanned the blackness, searching for obstacles. "I can't see much of anything. How 'bout you?"

"I'm afraid not." Grace tested her leg and then steadied her weight there. "I think my leg's better though. I believe I can walk."

"You sure?" Anne asked, still combing the air. She blinked a half-dozen times and her eyes began to adjust. Tall, thin trees with gnarled branches began to appear further in the distance. A few dark masses, like those she'd seen on several trees just inside the Mound's entrance, materialized as if by magic.

"Yes, I'm sure," Grace replied. She inched forward with both arms stuck out like Frankenstein's monster, swatting at the air around her. "But where'd the old man go? Can you see him?"

"Nope." Anne panned the darkness again, knowing his tuft of white hair would be impossible to miss.

"Well, then," Grace trailed, continuing forward. A revolting slosh came from underfoot as she stepped into the mire and forged ahead. Anne fell in behind her, wincing as her right foot was swallowed up by muck. "Aw, nasty. Can't we go another way?"

"I just…I can't see," Grace admitted. She made a hard left and Anne copied. After a slight crest, Anne felt twigs massaging the soles of her shoes. They seemed to balance above the mud, making for drier ground.

"Hey, this is better," Anne decided, just before the branches gave way.

Cracks rang through the air as the mesh of branches beneath the girls snapped and sent them tumbling downward. Anne felt herself falling, falling, falling as rounded walls of mud whizzed by. When finally she hit bottom, all the air was knocked from her lungs. Her heart boomed in her ears.

A shower of dry leaves fell from above, covering the girls' bodies. Grace rolled onto her shoulder and bumped Anne's leg. "Anne, are you alright?" she pressed, wincing.

"Alright might be a stretch," Anne groaned, cupping her thigh. She pulled herself into a sitting position and began examining her body as best she could in the gloom. In the forest above, she'd seen as through dark sunglasses and now it was as though they'd been dipped in tar. She narrowed in on a shaft of moonlight that trickled in from the hole through which they'd fallen, and followed it like a trail of breadcrumbs. It led to the outline of the pit overhead, and as Anne's eyes traced the hole, a suspect crackling resonated there.

Grace stirred beside her. "Do you hear that?"

"Shhhh." Still fixed above, Anne looked on in horror as the outlines of two figures rose like specters and peered directly into the abyss.

Chapter Eight

Anne cinched her lips closed and stopped breathing altogether. She and Grace linked hands and became very still, their focus aimed on the open mouth of the pit. Amidst the gloom overhead, another object slithered into view. It was not only moving, but also descending into the hole. Inch by inch, it crept closer until it touched down a handful of feet away from them and then coiled into a pile. Grace crawled towards it with Anne closed behind. "'Tis a vine," she whispered through the darkness. Her head tilted to face upward. "I think they mean to pull us up."

"And then what?" Anne gulped, her eyes darting upward again.

Grace shrugged and decided, "We haven't many other options," before gripping the vine, which was immediately drawn taut. She looped one coil around her right foot, hugged the tether, and began inching slowly out of sight.

Anne's gulp reverberated off the cavern walls and returned to her with increased volume. "You sure about this?" she called, as the last of Grace's feet was consumed by blackness.

"Not really!" Grace shouted back, vanishing altogether.

Anne gawked upwards and her neck stiffened. Fixed on the

void into which her friend had disappeared, she listened to her own breathing. As the silent seconds ticked by her breaths came quicker and louder, until she worried they may drown out any sound from above. "Grace? Grace? Are you okay?" Anne's calls were like that of a wounded animal.

"It's alright. Come on up!"

Anne shivered as the slimy vine reemerged from the dark. She coiled it around her left foot and braced her weight against it, just as a tug resonated from the opposite end. Soon she was ascending, an endless wall of muck inching by as she rose up the shaft and finally emerged from it like a blind mole.

"Appears I can't let you girls out of my sight, even for a second." The voice was unfamiliar, but its owner was not. Despite his strangeness, Anne smiled at the sight of their ancient guide and his new raven companion. Still perched atop the old man's shoulder, Onyx had obviously produced the second shadowy head eclipsing their pit of despair.

"Ain't many of these Faerie traps left 'round, but leave it to you two to find one," the codger added, winking.

Anne dusted herself off and joined Grace, who was standing near the edge of the pit. The old man's frenzied eyes darted over the pair of them and then to the forest beyond. "We'd best go," he explained, teetering back and forth on his cane. "Must keep moving. And for goodness' sake, step where I step!"

Before Anne had drawn a breath to contest this, the geezer was swallowed up by the blackness. Only his shaggy white head remained, like a torch for her and Grace to follow. It zigged and zagged for several hundred feet, and the girls kept close behind. Then, in an instant, it was gone.

"What? Where'd he go? You see him?" Anne blinked into the black, all but blind without him to lead her.

"No," Grace replied, reaching out and latching onto Anne's right arm. "I don't see him anywhere."

A muffled pop sprang from the ground just a few feet ahead, and with it, came their navigator. "Here, come here," the old man called. He was waving from a hollow between two decayed cedar trees, and as the girls followed, they found another tunnel walled with thatched twigs beyond it. "Down here!"

Gramps lit off into the tunnel without another word. Leaping along with the aid of his cane, he negotiated several forks and off-shoots, while the girls maintained a close distance. After several leagues, they arrived at a small, round door made of the same woven branches that lined the passage. Light entered there and shined the way to their exit.

"Back in The Brown," the old man announced as he stepped into the sunlight. Onyx lifted from his shoulder and took flight, seemingly materializing from thin air.

Anne grabbed Grace's hand and pulled her into the muddy

brush. "I'm not losing him again," she declared with a huff.

They set out at a sprint, and decayed wood whizzed by in Anne's peripheral vision, melting together like chocolate fondue. Only footsteps behind the codger, Anne and Grace followed as he crested a large mound of earth. He stopped halfway up and paused to survey the forest below, his wily eyes darting left and right, and then left again. With his mop of crazy hair and half-naked as he was, he looked quite mad. Anne began to wonder if following him had been the right choice after all.

The old man's nostrils twitched and his eyes turned to slits. "Looks all clear," he decided, turning around and crouching down to face the earth. He gripped a large boulder that lay there and then muscled it aside to reveal a hidden hole. "In you go."

Anne's feet refused to move. She glanced at the gaping hole in the ground and then back at the gnarled mass of brush from which they'd just emerged. Sensing her friend's hesitation, Grace stepped around and shot back a look of reassurance. "Come on, let's go."

Somewhere amidst the brushy undergrowth, Anne felt certain she caught sight of a pair of inky eyes, and she quickly turned back towards the hole. "Yeah, okay," she said, lowering to her hands and knees and following Grace into the void. The corridor beyond was a near mirror of the tunnels they'd passed through earlier in the day, but it came to a much more abrupt end at a large, rounded room with woven wood lining it from wall to wall. Several large shelves jutted from inside its belly, and judging by the blankets of dented moss that covered them, Anne reasoned they must be makeshift beds. The old man picked up a lit candle from a large stump at the center of the room and approached them with it held just under his chin. Glow from the wick cast an orange haze over his wrinkled face, and Anne decided his head could double for an oversized peach pit.

"What forest ya come from?" he asked, his eyes bulging.

"Sorry?" Grace returned. She was standing too near him for Anne's tastes.

The old man came nearer. Even from her distance, Anne could smell a reek of filth on him. "I asked what forest ya come from. Pink? Crimson?" His beady eyes scanned Grace up and down. "Yer a bit young. How long have you traveled?"

Grace cocked her head sideways and stared dumbly back without uttering a word. In the silence, a grating noise filtered in from the tunnel, and all eyes turned there just as Onyx popped from the hole. He toddled over like a wind-up toy, crowing excitedly as he approached the old man. "Onyx, my friend!" the old-timer exclaimed, bending to pat the bird.

Grace darted over and snatched the raven up. "How do you know that name?" she growled. "How do you know my bird?"

The geezer's wrinkles bunched together as he stared at Grace and Onyx. "Your bird?" He began to wobble and had to steady himself with his cane. It seemed as if he'd outrun time, and all at once, it was catching up with him. "Why, this bird lay by my crib when I was just a babe. This bird is more mine than anyone's."

Grace's eyelids peeled backwards and her words left her. She clutched Onyx tight to her chest. A drip-drip-drip of water falling from the cave's roof onto the twigs below reverberated in the quiet. After a couple of minutes, her voice broke gently, "What…what did you say your name was?"

"I didn't." The codger was still studying her, but his expression had turned sour. "'Tis Jacob."

Onyx let out a squawk as Grace dropped him. "It can't be!" Her jaw dropped and her arms fell to her sides like limp noodles. "Jacob? Jacob Rowden?"

A half-dozen of the old man's wrinkles vanished as his face drew tight. "I haven't heard that name in a very long time," he said at a whisper, adding a nod of affirmation.

For a moment, Grace hesitated, watching him as if studying an equation. Then a flash lit her eyes and she rushed at him and leapt like an attacking puma. "It's me," she stammered, grappling to hold him as he wriggled. "It's Grace! Your sister!" With her arms squeezed tightly around his midsection she blubbered, "I can't believe it! I can't believe you're alive! It all makes sense now!"

Jacob stopped fighting and grew rigid, arms pinned to his sides. His face flushed redder and redder, as if he were a tube of toothpaste being squeezed to the top.

"Oh, my dear brother! I feared I'd never see you again!" Grace buried her face in Jacob's bony chest, and mud painted her from one cheek to the other.

Still as stone, Jacob studied the dark swarm of locks nuzzling his bare skin just as Onyx joined them. Saddling Grace's shoulder, the raven swayed back and forth, all the while peering at Jacob. His stare had a warming effect and melted away several more wrinkles.

"But what of the others? Mother? Father? John? All of the townsfolk?" Grace asked, each word racing the next. She released her filthy brother and stood back, with arms still open wide.

Jacob sucked in a long breath, as if he'd been starving for air in the confines of Grace's embrace. "There are no others…not for a long while. They've all gone to the earth."

"The earth?" Grace's arms fell.

Anne shuffled close to her friend and softly explained, "I think he means they're dead."

"B-but—."

"Think about it, Grace…" Anne trailed. She cupped Grace's clammy hands and moved to face her. "It's been almost ninety years."

Anne sidestepped until the path between brother and sister was clear. "I mean, just look at Jacob. What was he — like a year old, when you saw him last?"

Fat tears welled at the corners of Grace's eyes and toppled over one another until they spilled down her cheeks. "So they're gone… they're all gone. And I am this!" she exclaimed, motioning fiercely towards herself and then digressing into sobs.

Jacob watched her with the wonder of a small child and innocently asked, "And what is this?"

"If only I knew!" Grace choked before collapsing into a pile on the ground, where she began to wail violently.

Jacob recoiled and several of the ruts returned to his brow. He retreated to the far wall of the cavern where he made a clatter, shuffling wooden mugs and a pitcher. An open flame backlit his chore, at the completion of which he returned with two steaming cups. "Here, drink this. It will calm yours nerves."

Dried of tears, Grace accepted her drink and downed it all in one swig. "Mmm, delicious!"

Anne drew her own mug close to her nose and breathed in an earthy scent. The drink was dark brown, like the kind of coffee her dad brewed when he had to get up very early in the morning. "It's good, Anne," Grace encouraged, nodding as she held her mug out for a refill. "I promise!"

Anne lifted the cup to her lips and sipped. "Hey, not bad!" she admitted. Soon after, she'd requested seconds herself.

Once they'd warmed their bellies, all three settled in a circle with Onyx at its center. "He all but dive-bombed me," Jacob explained, watching as candlelight shined on the raven's feathers. "But

I recognized him no time. My memories of him are fuzzy, but John went on about him so often."

Basking in his spotlight, Onyx turned several times like a model on a catwalk, and then lay down in the twigs. He looked on content-edly as Jacob continued. "He was carrying on, trying to get my at-tention…kept pecking at my toes and then dashing off, wanting me to chase him. And, of course, he led me right to you."

Anne chuckled. "Yeah, just in time too. Between that funky plant and those things, we were pretty hosed!"

Jacob stared at the far wall, curling his beard. "Well, the forest hasn't had a taste of life in a long time. I 'spect you'll find many things biting at you, draining you. Much worse in The Black, though. It'd suck the life clean out of you."

"The Black?" Grace breathed. She was hunched over with her eyelids drooping.

"Indeed, The Black Forest. Of course 'twas once the Olive, but it's gone dark with no life to feed it on the other side." Jacob was studying his sister, whose head continued to dip like a snagged fish-ing lure. "The Olive was our forest, the one connected to our town. But as with all the Faerie forests, it feeds from the humans who live on the other side of it. They like to make us think it's them who feed us, but one can't prosper without the other. When all life went dark on our side, its sister, here, did as well."

Grace nodded, her eyes now fully closed. She continued on

rocking, her head dipping lower and lower, until it finally came to rest beside Onyx on the floor. Following a groan, she curled into a ball and drifted off.

While watching her friend, Anne felt her own lids grow heavy and wondered if she was actually tired or just infected by Grace's weariness. Eyes half-closed, she craned towards Jacob and asked, "So how many forests are there, exactly?" Her words sounded far away as she spoke.

"Oh, there's a full dozen, just like Mr. Lang wrote. He named them, you know—his Faerie books—named each of them after one of the forests. His "Blue Fairy Book," "Crimson Fairy Book," "Olive Fairy Book"…named for The Brown Forest, The Crimson Forest, The Olive—err, Black Forest—and so on." Jacob chuckled to himself, crow's feet denting his temples. "He made such a big fuss about how he hadn't written all those Faerie stories, just edited them. Land's sakes, who'd make a better editor for a bunch of Faerie stories than a Changeling!"

Anne nodded, her head sagging. The rug of reeds below her legs looked so inviting. Perhaps she would lie down, just for a short while. Her eyes were so very dry. Closing them would be like heaven. Spooned alongside Grace on the floor, she watched the darkness play across her eyelids, and murmured, "Mmmm…the books I saw in your house…in the town…on the landing…before I fell… I remember…the fairy riding the toad." As desperately as she wanted to ask more, her lips were too exhausted to part.

As the black of sleep consumed Anne, she thought she heard Jacob whisper, "I'm sorry."

* * *

Bang! Bang! Bang!

Anne awoke with a start and was greeted by the image of Jacob dancing before her like a prospector, clapping a wooden spoon into the side of a pitcher. When he noticed she'd woken, he leapt towards her and drew his face very near. A smell of compost drifted in with him and as he squinted at her, his pupils reduced to razors. His upper lip curled until it nearly touched the tip of his hooked nose, and he muttered, "Hmmm," while still burrowing with his milky stare.

Grace's voice was insistent as she appeared over her brother's shoulder, also examining Anne's eyes. "She's alright, see? I told you, she's no Changeling."

"What? What the heck are you talking about?" Anne scooted back and struggled to her feet. Her legs felt as though they'd failed to wake with the rest of her body and she stumbled a bit as she came to stand.

Grace rushed to her side, explaining, "Just give it a moment. It takes a bit to wear off."

Jacob grinned sheepishly and hobbled towards them, all the while balancing on his cane. "I'm sorry about that. I just had to be sure," he said, adding, "It's just a bit of Barish root. No harm in it at all. Just puts you to sleep, sets you to dreaming."

128

"What?" Anne sputtered, still finding her feet. "You drugged us?"

"He had to," Grace defended him, while grabbing Anne's right arm and lending her support. "It was the only way to make sure we weren't Changelings."

Anne pulled her arm away and fumbled backwards. Pinned in the corner, she glanced back and forth between Grace and Jacob like a wounded animal sizing up its predators.

"No, no…Anne, please. Just listen. He meant no harm. He just had to be certain we were, well, us."

Anne stayed rigid and quiet.

"Might I?" Jacob asked, approaching with slow steps. "The root, miss, it but helps you dream. Only in dream does the Changeling return to its forest, to its true self. Why, that's how ole' Mr. Lang was able to hide all of those years…publish all those books and become a scholar in society. He hid in his human body, just as so many others have." Jacob snarled and then continued. "Clever gits they are, come into a body with all its memories and ready to spread their deception."

Anne stared on dumbly, too confused to speak.

With a glint of fire illuminating his eyes, Jacob continued, "But we know their secret! We've always known how to sort 'em out!" He came nearer and his tone dropped, as if he were parlaying a password in questionable company. "You have to catch 'em when they're deep in dream, and wake 'em while their soul is still in their world.

Then! Then you'll see!"

"See what?" Anne inched forward, curiosity overpowering her fear.

Jacob came closer still. The wiry hairs of his beard reached out towards Anne, nearly touching her. "Those eyes," he hissed, "those black, soulless eyes. Even in those human bodies, you wake 'em as they dream and their eyes will be black as pitch!"

A shudder ripped through Anne's body.

"Do you see, Anne? Do you understand now?" Grace asked, drifting near her friend.

Anne nodded and felt her heartbeat slow.

His eyes still fiery, Jacob maintained his closeness. "They're nasty little sprites…not to be trusted. Always playin' their little tricks, always up to no good." He stomped his cane on the ground and huffed off to the other side of the hollow. "We'd best stay put here a while. I 'spect they know you're here by now. Probably right outside, waiting."

"R-r-r-really?" Anne stuttered, backing away from her spot near the open hole through which they'd come. She bumped Grace and linked their arms. "What makes you think they won't come down here, then?"

Only clanking answered back as Jacob busied himself in his makeshift kitchen. Anne cleared her throat and glared at him. "Jacob?"

"Sorry?" Jacob dug in his ear while squeezing one eye closed.

"The Faeries…what makes you think they won't come down here?" Anne repeated, huddling closer to Grace.

"Oh, don't worry a bit about that. Faeries are born of the earth and only return there to die. They'd sooner swim in the Red Mountain than go underground!" He chuckled to himself before adding, "Stupid beasts!"

"The Red Mountain?" Grace asked. Her wary eyes were still trained on the cave's entrance.

"Indeed! That's the volcano at the center of the Red Forest. I've never seen it, mind you, but I've heard tell it's quite a sight!" With his back to them, Jacob's dirty buttocks shone through his moss undergarments, and Anne averted her eyes as he explained. "It's filled with a great pool of cherry-red lava. Must be quite a sight indeed!" When he turned towards the girls again, Jacob's eyes glowed as if he were gazing at the magnificent volcano in his mind's eye. "Would've been somethin' to see it," he trailed, his tone softening.

"Why didn't you?" Grace asked, now studying her brother rather than the hole leading outside. His head had begun to dip as if carrying a great weight.

Jacob perked up, and the haze that had settled over his eyes cleared. "Oh, 'tis far too great a distance. It'd take a lifetime, or so I've been told."

"Wow, really?" Anne interjected, moving to join Grace, whose drawn her within feet of Jacob.

"Oh, yes," he replied. "The forests are vast. Their portals link up all over the world, you know. They're all connected by The Grey, of course, but unless they share a narrow border, you're unlikely to travel between them, unless you forfeit years of your life to the journey."

Anne turned towards Grace, whose focus was still pinned on her brother. "The Grey, that'd be the forest we arrived at. Remember how everything looked all dead and grey, even the sun?"

"Indeed, it did," Grace agreed.

Jacob made a slow nod. "That'd be it. All portals empty to The Grey. But where you arrive depends entirely upon what forest you've come from." He scratched at his chin and stared hard at Grace. "You musta traveled for a time in The Grey, eh?" Grace bobbed her head, to which he responded, "That explains why I first found you in The Brown."

"So, great then. We just get back to The Grey and we can hop a portal back home!" Anne rejoiced. Much as she feared the Faerie that lay outside, she feared her aunt far more. By now, Claudia had surely come unhinged.

Jacob cleared his throat and turned away from the girls. "Oh no, you can't go back...not ever. The forest will never let you leave." His words seemed to hang in the air above Anne's head, looping over and over again like a record. She stared upward in a dumbstruck daze as if watching them.

"What do you mean we can't leave?" Grace asked, her voice aquiver. She moved towards Jacob, who had once again busied himself in the ramshackle kitchen and was muttering gibberish. "Jacob, what do you mean? What do you mean by that?"

Jacob jerked around suddenly. Caught off guard, Grace stumbled back a few steps and nearly fell. "I mean we can't leave. None of us! EVER!" he shouted. His eyes were suddenly fierce. "That's how it is. That's how it's always been! The forest won't have it!"

Shaken by his explosion, Anne broke from her stupor. "Won't have it? C'mon, what's the forest really gonna do?"

"Plenty," Jacob growled back. "We tried...believe me, we tried." His body hunched, revealing a pronounced backbone. As he continued, his tone was gentler. "You can't though. You can't go back out. We are like food to the mouth of the portal. It's a bit of a one-way ticket." Bearing heavily upon his cane, he made his way towards one of the sleeping pads carved in the cave wall and sat down upon it with a sigh.

Grace shadowed her brother's steps with Anne close behind. "So...so the portal won't let us back through? It won't allow us passage out?" she asked while pulling nervously at her hair.

Jacob shook his head and cast his eyes to the earth. He drew his legs up on the ledge and they sunk into the thick moss there. "Never. It'll never let you out," he trailed in a wistful way, staring into nothing. He was still for a time. His cloudy eyes were fixed on some spot on the wall, but he eventually lay down and closed them.

Chapter Nine

Jacob's snores filled the cavern. Loud and restless as they were, Anne imagined earth shaking from the walls as they rumbled back and forth. The girls had found sleeping pads of their own, but with minds abuzz and a freight train for a roommate, they both lay wide awake.

"Grace, you awake?" Anne quietly asked.

Grace peeked over the side of her ledge, her almond-shaped eyes like silverfish in a dark stream. "Very."

Jacob made a loud snort and turned on his side, to face the wall.

"I was thinking," Anne began, sitting up so that her head was just a few inches from the bottom of Grace's pad. "What if Jacob is a Changeling?"

Grace scrunched her nose and made a quick jerk of her head. "That's ridiculous."

"No, really. I mean…we don't know. He could totally be lying. Maybe he's not your brother at all." Anne looked over her shoulder at Jacob. His backside was heaving in the darkness, as the dying flames of candlelight licked at it. "Maybe that whole thing about not being able to leave, maybe that's all a load of crap, too. Maybe he's trying to keep us here until his Faerie buddies show up so they can suck us up, or wear us as people suits, or whatever the heck it is they do."

Grace became very still. After a few moments, she reanimated and asked, "Well, then, why did he save us?"

"I dunno," Anne replied, falling briefly into quiet speculation. "Maybe he wanted us all for himself?"

Grace rolled onto her back with a groan and mumbled, "Ridiculous, just ridiculous," at little more than a whisper.

"No, no. I can totally see it. It totally makes sense. I mean, how would he have lived here all this time and not gotten nabbed?" Anne slung her legs to the ground and a soft crunch rose from her feet.

Grace's face materialized like a Cheshire cat's alongside Anne's sleeping pad. Her eyes had narrowed. "What are you doing?" she hissed.

Anne made no reply but instead arched to tiptoes and began making her way towards Jacob. Passing the weakening candle, she carefully lifted it and approached his bedside with it held out in front of her. "I'm gonna test him. I'm gonna prove it to you."

"Anne, no!" Grace barked as angrily as her whisper would allow. She scaled her bunk and lowered into Anne's now-empty one.

An arm's length from Jacob, Anne could see his scraggly moustache vibrating along with his snores. As she made up the final step between them, a startling snap rang from below, where a twig had broken under the weight of her sneaker. Awakened by the sound, Jacob bolted upright like a mummy from the grave and began frantically punching at the air. His bright blue eyes bulged in the blackness, wild and veined with crimson.

Anne tumbled backwards and fell to the floor along with her candle. "Whoa, whoa! It's just me!"

Jacob was on his feet in an instant, his fists clenched. His wooly mane of hair stood on end, as if he'd just received an electric shock. "What? What?" His head jerked towards Anne's spot on the ground. "What were you doing, fool girl?"

Anne strained through the blackness, fixing on Jacob's Yeti-like shadow. "Sorry," she blubbered. "I just thought... I had to be sure."

"Sure of what?" Jacob asked, fumbling around a small upturned log near his sleeping area. Following a crisp scratch from the same location, the cave flooded with fresh candlelight. The flame lit his face and a heavy brow.

Tongue-tied, Anne looked on in silence as Grace emerged from the shadows, Onyx tucked under her arm like a loaf of rye bread, and replied on her behalf. "She had this silly idea, Jacob. She thought you might be a—"

"A what?" Jacob asked.

Anne felt her face reddening, and she cast her eyes to the floor. "A Changeling, okay? I thought you might be a Changeling. I had to check. I'm sorry."

Jacob fell quiet, studying her. The drip in the cavern ceiling seemed to resume in that instant and the trio sat in shared silence, listening helplessly as it consumed the quiet. Deciding she'd formulate a more gracious apology, Anne lifted her eyes and found Jacob wearing a nearly toothless grin. "Ha! Ha!" he rollicked, his sudden eruption booming through the cave. "That's it, girl! That's the way! Only way to survive in this place…always be on your guard!"

A smile warmed Anne's face. With one eyebrow cocked she peered at Grace, who duplicated her dumb grin and shrugged.

"Well, it was a fine idea!" Jacob bellowed, clutching his concave belly. "But I'm afraid there's no chance o' that. After all, only the willing can be transformed into a Changeling!"

Still silent, Grace studied Jacob with her head tilted sideways. With her mass of dark hair drawn to the side, she resembled a confused, one-eared Cocker Spaniel that Anne had once seen on "Animal Planet." Jacob shifted towards his sister, paused briefly, and added, "I most certainly didn't come through that hell-gate of my own will!"

"Oh, I didn't realize that's the way it worked," Anne said, resisting the urge to offer her friend a milk bone.

"Well, you wouldn't." Jacob replied in a low voice. His smile ran like candle wax, dripping into a frown. He peered at the ceiling and strained, as if burrowing through the earth. "That's why they don't like to take us as they did. Can't take a man's will; he's got to give it. Take us in a big heap as they did — take us without consent — and they can't work their evil charms." His frown lifted, forming a rigid line across his face. After growling, he added, "That's why they want the offering…make it like it was our idea in the first place."

Jacob's features fell as his voice was overshadowed by the sound of a low throb, like a heaving heart, that trickled from the shadows. Tracing it to the source, Anne found Grace quietly sobbing. "Oh, how they took you…took you all. Oh, how awful it must've been!" she sputtered, her cheeks glistening in the candlelight.

Anne approached her friend, who was clutching Onyx so tightly that his eyes bulged like ripe blackberries about to burst. "Shhhh, it's okay," Anne cooed.

"It was me. It was all me! They took you because of me!" Grace wailed.

"Now wait just one minute!" Jacob was suddenly spry, bouncing to his sister's side before Anne had even arrived. "Not one lick of that was your doing! You want to blame someone? Blame Father. He cut that enchanted tree. He carved that bewitched trunk. He put you inside it. He knew the Faerie'd never find you there." His hand now on Grace's shoulder, Jacob lowered his face so close to hers that they nearly brushed noses. "Said it was the best thing he ever did in all his days."

"Really?" Grace sputtered, raising her eyes to meet his.

"Really," Jacob replied, matter-of-factly. "And he was right. I was the best thing he ever did. Just knowin' that you were out there, that you were safe, that right there was the one thing that gave him hope…gave us all hope. It was the one thing that kept us going. And besides," he continued, now glaring daggers overhead, "those damn devils would'a had us all in here by now anyway. And had they got their way, each and every one of us would'a been turned into a monster while they were livin' in our bodies on the outside." He spat at the ground and raised a balled fist to the ceiling. "When my day comes, I'm gonna die a man!"

Witnessing their exchange, Anne pined for her family. The realization that she might never see them again came like a punch to the gut. She grew very still, soaking in the darkness and praying for a spark to light her way. Her epiphany exploded like a firework. "The Faeries…the ceremony…that's it!"

Grace and Jacob had embraced, but as Anne erupted, they parted. Onyx fell from the empty space left between them as if he were sliding from the windshield of a semi. Anne grinned at the sight of his disheveled feathers, and continued, "The Faeries, they leave the forests, right? They cross out of the portal to switch places with the offered child, right? So there must be some way to get out!"

Coldness settled over Jacob's features again as Grace left his arms. "Oh, there's a way," he mumbled. "But it's not for us."

"I don't understand. What do you mean, it's not for us?" Anne returned, folding her arms across her chest.

"Oh, you'll see."

* * *

It was near dusk when they'd gone underground, but as they emerged from the cave just a short while later the sun appeared as if it had just begun to rise. "Time works differently here," Jacob explained as the girls marveled at the sky. "There's a dozen forests and each has its own light: some from suns, some moons, some not quite one or the other. They speed up and slow down and never behave the same today as they did yesterday." Glaring at the orb cresting the horizon he added, "Ask me, it's done to drive us all batty."

Anne dropped her eyes from the sky just in time to see Jacob's bare, bony thighs consumed by the underbrush. He sniffed at the air like a bloodhound on the trail of a fox and jogged towards a trail to his right.

"C'mon," Anne said, nudging Grace, who still gaped overhead as if star-struck. "We don't wanna get behind."

"Oh, of course," Grace half-mumbled, notching her fingers through Anne's. The girls set off at gallop and quickly caught up to Jacob. He'd mashed a good deal of the brush down with his cane, and it made for easier traveling. In twenty minutes they'd covered a half-mile but progress stopped as Jacob froze and held his arms out in front of them, crossing guard-style.

"What the—?" Anne grumbled, her head level with his rancid armpit.

"Shhhh!" Jacob scanned the forest before them, moving not a muscle. "I hear something," he whispered. Ears a-twitch, his eyes darted between several trees and then to a thicket just beyond. Creeping slowly, he told the girls, "Follow me. Keep quiet," and inched towards the western-most tree. Its trunk was enormous and all three of them piled behind it, easily hidden from sight of the thicket on the other side. There, just beyond the underbrush, were three Faeries lain out on the ground. Each of their heads rested on a large boulder, and sheets of tree bark covered their bodies like blankets. Though their eyes remained open, each lay as if sleeping, making peculiar grumbling noises that resembled snores.

Grace craned over Jacob's left shoulder and drew her lips near his ear. "What are they doing?" she murmured.

"Playin'. Pretendin'." Jacob replied, just as softly.

"The others we saw. They were pretending, too, like they had a fire. They had bowls, but no soup. They warmed their hands with no flame," Grace offered, her sights fixed on the creatures.

Jacob nodded. "Yeah, they do it a lot. They dream of bein' human. That's all they ever do." He made a low chuckle. "Kinda funny, if you think on it. Little kids runnin' around, playin' like they're fairies, and here the Faerie are, pretendin' to be human."

"Aw," Anne fussed. "Poor things."

Jacob jerked his head to the right, positioning his eyes but an inch from Anne's. "Oh, no, you don't," he snarled. "Don't you go feelin' sorry for them. They get hold of ya and play house with ya for a while, and you won't pine for 'em no more." His eyes grew dark, haunted by the specters of his memory. "Seen many a friend fall to such a fate."

Anne began, "Oh, I—" but cut herself short as sounds of a scuffle trickled through the bushes. In an instant, all eyes returned to the thicket where one of the beings, by far the largest of the three, had risen and was kicking the Faerie who lay nearest him. Still pretending to sleep, the smaller creature rocked back to his original position every time he was hit. After a third punt, his head twisted to the side, and he locked eyes with his aggressor. They remained like that for several minutes, before Anne whispered, "Now what are they up to?" at Jacob.

"Probably arguin', I 'spect."

Grace still spied over her brother's shoulder, and observed aloud, "But they aren't talking," as much to herself as anyone else.

"Oh no, no mouths…no talkin'. They do it with their minds."

"Ooh, like telepathy?" Anne asked without turning to face Jacob.

"No, I don't think so. Not exactly, anyway." Jacob answered back while adjusting his crouched position. "Way I always heard it, they speak to each other in pictures." After a short snort, he added, "Dullards. Probably wouldn't know a word from a turd!"

Anne stifled a giggle and looked on as the bossy Faerie triumphed and lowered his lanky body onto the mat where his comrade had been only moments ago. Though his face remained expression-less, Anne sensed a certain satisfaction in his features as he settled in and pulled up his bark blanket. Meanwhile, his ousted friend wan-dered to a nearby tree stump and quietly sat down.

"Best watch yourself there," Jacob warned just as Anne felt something abrasive being dragged down her pant legs. She turned to trace the source and instantly froze. Tentacles of climbing moss had engulfed her sneakers and were inching up her legs. They bore bright green tips that almost glowed against their dank surroundings. "Don't move," Jacob warned, looping his cane through the swath and giving a hard tug. The tentacles curled back, and Anne was cer-tain she heard a soft squeal surface as they did so.

"Eww!" Anne pulled her legs up close to her chest and free of the moss, but the lively tentacles pursued her, gripping at the ground as would the fingers of someone hanging from a precipice. "Jacob! Help!" she wailed.

With a swish of his cane, Jacob looped the whole swath like a plate of spaghetti noodles and hoofed it into the brush.

"And that," he puffed, leering into the brush, "is why we always keep moving. Damn forest'll eat'chya alive." He held his finger to his lips and motioned back towards the trail. "We got a ways to go, anyway. C'mon. And keep quiet!"

Hand in hand, Anne and Grace backed away from the thicket

with wary eyes covering their footsteps. A few leagues out, they turned and followed after Jacob, who'd already vanished into The Brown. "This way," Anne decided, sniffing the air. "I think I can smell him!"

In moments, Jacob's white mop came into view, the shadow of Onyx's spread wings slicing it in two. As the girls neared him, Jacob announced, "He's a clever one," while watching as the raven soared overhead. "John used to tell us stories about him and all the things ya'll trained him to do." Smiling weakly, he continued, "Does me good to see him again," and then fell quiet. In the silence, his huffs boomed as he quickened his pace.

Anne's moss-mauled leg still ached, and she found herself struggling to keep up. She trailed behind her two traveling companions as the hours dragged on, catching up to Grace only when she snagged her dress on bits of brush. Each path looked the same: brown and dead, as if they'd entered into the land of perpetual winter. After several miles of it, Anne felt she might go mad if she didn't see another color soon. The prospect of lying down and allowing an aggressive vine to overtake her simply to see it turn green had become disturbingly appealing. "How much further?" she finally whined.

Jacob was still puffing up ahead. "Nearly there, girl, nearly there," he promised between pants. He pointed at a rise in the earth a football field's length away, and said, "Just over that ridge."

The slope was farther away than it had originally appeared, and as they began to climb it, the sun dipped beneath the opposite side and set them in near darkness. "I can't see a thing!" Grace bellowed, sliding in the wet earth that coated the hill. Moving alongside her, Anne also struggled for traction, and the girls linked hands, trying to help one another up.

"Watch me! Follow me!" Jacob turned his shoeless feet outward, as would a duck, and began scaling the hill at a good pace. The girls imitated and soon found their path an easier one. After several falls, a couple trips, and one face-plant, all three arrived at the top of the ridge breathless and covered head to toe in mud.

Anne gaped through dirt-crusted eyelids at the view before them. On the other side of the ridge lay a steep drop, plummeting several hundred feet. It ended at a sharp cliff, and the chasm beyond it was so dark and so vast that she could not see its end. A few car lengths from the cliff, a mass of land cropped up from the chasm. It was oval in shape and no bigger than the footprint of her two-story house back in Alberta. Not unlike an island, it seemed to spring from the abyss and had no connecting terrain. A few bare trees sprang like enormous skeleton hands from the earth, their branches pointing like fingers into the darkening sky. Even from a distance, Anne could make out bodies milling amidst the trees, and asked, "Are they Faeries?"

"Aye. Well, in a manner of speaking, anyhow," Jacob replied. He clutched both the girls' shoulders and pushed down with his gnarled hands. "Better tuck down a bit. Even from here, they could spy us."

146

Muck squished beneath them as the girls hunkered down in the mud, forced to rest on their elbows. Anne winced and asked, "What do you mean, in a manner of speaking? They look like Faeries to me." She peered over the slope at the crest of the hill, tracking one of the beings as he walked from one side of the island to the other.

"Well, they're Faerie all right, but they're also not."

Anne grumbled and shot Jacob a look of reproach.

A playful twinkle lit his eyes, as Jacob explained, "They're Offerings: once-human Faeries." He looked out over the canyon and studied them, his eyes turning dull. "Slaves, really. 'Spose you could consider 'em second-class citizens. Any of the Faeries that got a human soul inside 'em are destined to servitude. They're as good as dogs here."

"One, two, three, four, five, six. I see six of them down there." Anne rubbed at her face, where dirt had begun to dry and tickle her skin. "So if they're slaves…what are they slaving at? Looks to me like they're just standin' around."

Jacob was still staring out over the ravine. "They're guarding," he whispered, quickly shifting his attention to the ground just behind them, where Onyx had set down with a quiet thump.

The raven waddled over to Grace and she cupped her hand over his back. "Guarding what?" she asked.

"Only the most precious thing in all the forest," Jacob purred, his pupils swelling. "The Talisman." Fixed on some spot in the distance, his eyes glassed over. "With it, the portal will release you. With it, you're free."

A spark ignited deep in Anne's chest. She studied the Faeries milling about their island, and excitedly asked, "Have you tried—?" but was interrupted by a groan from Jacob.

"Yes. More times than I can count. We've tried every which way to cross that chasm. The island gullies 'round here are lined with the bones of my friends..." He turned to his sister and wistfully added, "...my family," following which Grace gulped and bit her lip. "No, the Faerie are the only ones likely to make use of that Talisman. They've made certain of that." His eyes turned steely. "After all, how do you defeat an enemy who never sleeps? Never eats? Who can guard one spot for all his days?" As he turned away, Jacob sighed. "As I told you, while there's a way, it's no way for us."

Anne continued inspecting the Faerie island, despite the sensation that she was only tempting herself with a treat that would always lie just out of reach. Overhead, the sun resumed its hasty descent into the earth, until it was only a husk on the horizon. As it vanished from sight, blackness consumed the Faerie's bodies one by one. When only two remained, Anne mumbled, "So, they're trapped there? Just as trapped as we are here?"

"Mmmm, I suppose so," Jacob replied while pushing himself upright. "We'd best find somewhere to ride out the night. I think there are some digouts still intact nearby."

He set off on a downhill descent with stiff heels that scooped out divots in the mud. "Walk this way," he called, fading into The Brown. "You're gonna have to learn the tricks of getting by 'round here, if you expect to stay alive."

Chapter Ten

Jacob's "digout" was another twig-lined hole in the earth, although it was much smaller than the one in which he made his home. It had been abandoned for some time and lacked a certain warmth. Anne and Grace huddled close together, their only blanket the dried mud that covered the better part of both of their bodies. It was difficult to sleep and several hours passed before Anne's body succumbed to exhaustion. She slept restlessly, haunted by dark dreams, and when she woke it seemed fitting that the digout was still inky black inside. She cleared her throat, stretched, and made a soft yawn.

"Sun's still not up," Grace said at a whisper. She was facing the round hole through which they'd entered. "It's been forever, and it's still not up." Her voice was weary. Anne wondered if she'd slept at all.

Anne stared hard at the entrance until its outline appeared like that of an eclipsed moon. "Must be temperamental today," she offered. Her stomach made a low growl, and she grimaced. "Jeez, how long has it been since we've eaten?"

"I can't remember," Grace admitted, still staring at the hole. The curtain of black rippled slightly as Onyx emerged from it, like a 3D image come to life. He sailed in and landed near the center of the small room, dropping something on the ground beneath him as he did so. After a few seconds, he made a loud caw that awoke Jacob and set the codger upright on his sleeping pad.

"What's all that about?" Jacob grumbled, swinging his feet from the ledge on which he'd made his bed. Onyx hopped towards the old man and then back to the spot at which he'd landed, dancing around the item he'd dropped. Jacob followed behind and once close to the object, he dropped to his knees and grabbed it up. "Good bird, good bird!" he echoed. Jacob rose and held a dead rat out for the girls to see. "Look what this dandy bird has brought us!" he exclaimed with a manic grin.

Grace winced and said, "Oh. How lovely."

The girls looked on as Jacob approached a large stone near the center of the room and unsheathed a homemade knife from the waistband of his mossy drawers. He proceeded to skin the rat while smacking his chapped lips, and then, setting it aside, pulled a candle and some flint from a hole hidden beneath his sleeping shelf and used it to spark a small fire on the top of the rock.

With a worrisome wink at his spectators, he next tore a foot-long twig from the lining of the cave and rammed it up the rat's backside until it emerged out the unfortunate creature's nose. Skinless and skewered, Jacob held the body over the open flame, smiling all the while. "Looks good and done," he purred after just a few minutes. "What end do you two want?"

"I'll pass, brother," Grace gulped and cupped her mouth.

Anne pointed at Jacob. "It's all yours."

"Suit yourself!" Jacob declared with a widening smile. He gnashed his two remaining teeth at the carcass and consumed everything but the head and bones in a matter of seconds. Following a moan of satisfaction, he tossed the thumb-sized head at Onyx's feet, chanting, "Good bird, good bird," again.

Onyx examined the meat, pecked it a few times, and then hopped up beside the girls on their sleeping pad. "He is a good bird," Grace praised, patting his silky back. "So clever."

"Yeah, he really is." Anne added, watching as Grace's ivory fingers slid down Onyx's back and then returned to his crown, only to repeat the motion again and again. It lulled her into a daze of sorts and Anne focused hard on the raven until her mind drifted to a path of its own choosing. After a few moments of mental meandering, her eyes lit with such ferocity that they could have illuminated the entire forest. "Onyx! That's it! Onyx can save us!" She leapt from the ledge and immediately began pacing the dim cave. "I can't believe I didn't think of it before! He got us a rat…" Anne looked at the teeny head still lying in the middle of the cave and muscled down an upsurge of vomit before continuing, "…why couldn't he get us the talisman?"

Anne dashed towards Jacob and then stooped to bring their eyes level, while trying to ignore the bit of gut drying on his lower lip.

"You said John trained him, right? You said he trained Onyx to do all kinds of stuff, right?"

Jacob dumbly nodded and the entrails dropped from his lip to the ground below.

"Well, why couldn't we train him? Couldn't we just train him to fly over that big ravine and snatch up the talisman?" Anne frantically asked. Eyes wide, she hurried towards Grace, who was still hanging from their sleeping pad with Onyx in her lap. "I mean, those Faeries wouldn't even see it comin', ya know? He could swoop right in there and snatch it before they even saw him." Anne pointed towards the still darkened doorway, and added, "Heck, it's so dark here, most of the time, that he'd practically be invisible!"

Grace bobbed her head. "Yeah, I guess it could work."

"What do you mean could work? It's perfect!" Anne swung her head back towards Jacob, gesturing excitedly. "It's perfect, right?"

Jacob was quiet. He rose slowly, returned to his sleeping ledge and perched on the edge. Fingering his chin, he modeled a blank stare for a minute or two, and then decided, "Yeah, I 'spose it could work."

"See, Grace, even your brother thinks it'll work!" Eyes sparkling, Anne returned her focus to Grace, who had resumed stroking Onyx. Grace didn't look up. "Grace! Did you hear him? We're gonna get out of here!"

"What does it matter?" Grace asked, still staring at her lap.

"Even if we do return, there's nothing left for me. My family, my friends…they're all gone. And even if we manage to make it back, I'll be trapped in that town for all my days." Her tone was wistful, and as she finished speaking, a tear dropped from her face and melted into Onyx's feathers.

Anne stopped pacing, plopped down on the floor and began chewing her lip. Her shoulders slumped and the cave fell still.

Jacob voice was like the creak of a slow-opening door as it breached the silence. "You say you were trapped…on the other side?"

Nodding, Grace replied, "Yes, I couldn't leave the town," without looking up.

"We couldn't get her past the Faerie ring," Anne explained. "Her or her journal. Any time either attempted to cross the ring, they got held back." She stared at the carpet of twigs beneath her and began tracing the outline of a necklace there with her fingertip, similar in shape to how she imagined the talisman.

"Mmmmm," Jacob trailed. He had progressed from fiddling with his chin to massaging his forehead. "Bewitched, I 'spose, from that long stay in the Faerie trunk. Either that or the nasty lil' sprites put a hex on ya when they spirited us away." He stopped his kneading and looked up. "Either way, I'd think that talisman would get ya past the ring. It's a bit like a magic key."

Grace's head lifted, her eyes brightened. "Truly? Do you truly

154

think so?" she asked, her voice climbing several octaves.

"Aye," Jacob replied through a surly grin. For a fleeting moment Anne imagined him with a peg leg and an eye patch, Onyx swaying atop his shoulder in rhythm with the high seas.

"Oh, my!" Grace exclaimed before racing across the room and leaping into her brother's arms. After a brief embrace, she flew to Anne and hugged her tightly as well.

"I think you forgot somebody," Anne said with a chuckle. She pointed at Onyx, who was stumbling around beneath the girls' sleeping ledge, where Grace had unwittingly tossed him in her excitement.

"Sorry, sorry, sorry," Grace sputtered. She returned to the dazed raven and scooped him up. "You wonderful, marvelous, clever, handsome bird!" she sang, spinning him around. "You'll save us! I just know you will!"

* * *

The sun refused to wake for several more hours, but the girls didn't mind. They tucked themselves around Jacob's candlelight and talked of all the things they would do once Grace was free of her prison.

"Oh, and I can't wait to take you to a movie!" Anne exclaimed as light began to trickle in from outside.

"I've seen a moving picture. It was amazing! I saw 'The Man in the Moon'! Grace's eyes sparkled as she spoke.

155

"Trust me, Grace, you ain't seen nothin' yet!" Anne teased, grinning. Her face had begun to ache from prolonged smiling, and it was almost a relief when it fell as her attentions were drawn towards Jacob, whose steady snores of the last several hours broke and progressed to a series of snorts as he shifted restlessly on his sleeping ledge.

"Well then, there she comes," he said, as he awoke and greeted the sun, while squinting at the passage leading outside. He righted himself on the bench, scratched the back of his head and added, "Better get goin'. We don't know how long she'll stick around today."

His hair was a wild mess. Anne smiled at the sight of him and her cheekbones ached. "Where we headed?" she asked.

Jacob stood, located his cane, and began hobbling towards the exit. "Back to my digout, of course. Didn't you say you wanted to get goin' on trainin' this bird?" He motioned towards Onyx and gave Anne a grumpy glare. "Got everything I oughta need back there."

"But—" Anne sputtered, "but then don't we just have to come all the way back here again?" Her face drooped as she revisited their hike. "I mean, why go all the way back to your digout when we only have to turn around and come right back again to get the talisman?"

Grace stood and folded her arms across her chest. Her features had grown stony. "I agree, Jacob. It makes no sense!"

Jacob made a half-chuckle that came out as a sniff. "Yeah, that wouldn't make no sense 'tal, if we were comin' back here. But we ain't." He looked over his shoulder and gestured towards the island they'd visited the night prior. "That talisman out there ain't the one you need. That key belongs to The Brown and us, we come from The Black." He finished out his chuckle, then added, "You take that talisman and who knows where you'd end up!"

The girls stared at him, both silent and still, willing him with their expectant eyes to continue. Jacob shifted his weight onto his cane and explained, "Ya see, each forest has its own talisman; its own magic key. The Brown's talisman is gonna get you outta the Brown, so you're gonna end up wherever it is that The Brown links up on the other side. Could be halfway around the world…could be in another world altogether. No way of knowin'."

Anne's throat felt dry when she spoke again. "So we've gotta go get the talisman in The Black in order to get back out the same place we came in at?"

"Now you're gettin' it," Jacob praised with a nod.

Following a moan, Grace rolled up on her haunches, which woke Onyx. He rose on his matchstick legs and stumbled around as if inebriated. Grace watched him, her face expressionless, and decided, "Well then, let's get on with it."

She stood and Anne followed suit. Soon all three were bathing in the morning sun. The wretched Brown stretched out before them, an unwelcoming sight.

"Oh, joy." Anne inhaled a deep breath of stagnant air and started walking.

Jacob, already unsatisfied with her slow steps, hurried past and began zigzagging back and forth across their murky path. "The sun may seem a friend," he called back. "But just remember, if we can see better, we can better be seen!"

Grace's eyes widened as they met with Anne's, but she quickly diverted them and began panning the landscape. In a flash, her steps quickened and Anne mimicked her. They moved at a jackrabbit's pace and the hours passed by in a muddy flurry. By sunset, they'd arrived at Jacob's cave, and after a brief rest and a meal of seeds and berries, they set about training Onyx.

Using a handful of seeds, Grace lured the raven onto a stump set at the room's center, and all three studied him as he pecked away at the pile. "Okay, so how did John train him?" Anne asked, watching as Onyx inhaled the BB-sized seeds.

"I'm not entirely sure," Grace admitted. She turned towards her brother, who was leering at the seed as it vanished. "As I recollect, he used food…used it to reward him. Does that sound right, Jacob?"

Jacob's eyes bugged at the now-empty stump. "Yes, more food. More food is in order!" he declared. Entering the kitchenette, he unearthed a small sack of seeds and cradled it as if were an infant. Through the sack's top, he extracted two handfuls. One disappeared into his mouth and the second returned with him to the stump. "Now what?" he mumbled between engorged cheeks.

"You mean you don't know?" A vein popped from Anne's forehead.

Jacob's eyes dropped as he blubbered, "It's...it's been ages." He balled his fist and knocked on his head, as if it were a closed door. "Ole' memory ain't what it used to be."

Anne shook her head and held out a cupped hand. "Here, give me the seeds," she instructed. Jacob obeyed, unclenching his fingers, as would a rusted tin man. He poured a golden stream into her waiting palm and watched each granule fall as if it were painful.

"Okay," Anne began, "now we need something that looks like the talisman. Do you have anything like that, Jacob?"

Without a word, Jacob began scavenging the cave. Lifting little sections of the floor, he exposed several hidden cubbyholes, sometimes with a grumble and twice with an "Ahh!" After some shuffling about the kitchen, he returned to the stump holding a long piece of twine attached to a rectangular rock. "This oughta do," he decided, handing it to Anne.

"Yeah, okay. This'll work." Anne took the necklace and placed it on the stump, several inches from where Onyx was still perched. "I saw this on 'Animal Planet,'" she explained, hovering near the raven. "We've just gotta reward him every time he gets near that thing. Once he's doin' that, we make him earn it—make it so he's gotta pick it up before he gets a treat."

Grace's forehead dented. "You've seen a planet of only ani-mals? And they train ravens there?"

Sniggering, Anne kept her eyes on Onyx. "It's a TV show, Grace. Uh...kinda like a movie but in your house. And they didn't train ravens on it—they trained dogs to get the paper." Onyx ap-proached the imitation talisman and Anne readied her reward. "I fig-ure, if it'll work on a dog, it might work on a raven, too," she said.

Grace nodded and her eyes glazed. "Oh, I see," she lied, watch-ing as Onyx dipped his head and rotated it sideways, examining the necklace. He blinked, jerked his neck twice, and then inched for-ward.

"C'mon, c'mon," Anne purred as he drew nearer. He leveled his eyes at the stone and made a move to peck at the twine. When his beak made contact, Anne gently tossed a half-dozen seeds his way. He devoured them and then looked to her for more. "Oh, no, you don't. You've got to earn them," she teased, pulling her hand back. Onyx shot her a puzzled look and then returned his attention to the talisman. After examining it for a brief moment, he made a second peck, and again, Anne showered him with food.

Grace clapped from the sidelines and leaked a giggle.

"Shhhh!" Anne growled, eyes intent upon her student.

Onyx was undeterred by the interruption and began pecking mercilessly at the talisman, earning himself several more seeds.

Jacob glowered over Anne's shoulder. "You gotta give him so

much? That stuff ain't easy to come by, ya know!"

Anne glanced at her half-empty hand and then back at Onyx. "Okay birdie, you've got to do some thinkin' now. No more until you pick it up," she explained. Onyx was deaf to her words, continuing to peck at the twine, and then the rock, and back again. After several fruitless exercises, he raised his head and glanced from her face to her hand, as if trying to communicate his desires. "Nope, no more," she said, adding, "Better figure it out!"

"Perhaps he doesn't understand," Grace offered. "I mean to say, he's no dog."

"No, he'll get it. Just give him a chance." Anne clenched the seeds tightly in her palm, as Onyx stared on. Could a bird snarl? Following a final piercing glare, he slunk away from the talisman, but then quickly returned and began pecking it again, interspersing looks at Anne's hand. "Nope, that's not what I want. C'mon, Onyx, you can do this."

In his pecking fit, Onyx managed to snag a braid of twine around his beak and as he recoiled, it lifted. "Good boy! Good boy!" Anne exclaimed, tossing far too much seed at his feet. He greedily consumed it and danced about, as if applauding his own performance. After a few encores, he had an engorged belly and mind.

"I can't believe it worked!" Jacob admitted, crouching to retrieve several seeds that had fallen to the floor. He popped them into his mouth and made a groan of satisfaction.

Anne turned up her nose as she watched him. "Jeez, thanks for the vote of confidence." Glancing at her hand, she counted only a dozen or so seeds remaining. "But we're not done yet. Still gotta get him to fly somewhere to get the thing. That'll be the tricky part."

Jacob's bones made a creak as he rose to stand. His milky eyes focused on the raven and then upon Anne. "Nah, girl, the tricky part will be gettin' out of here alive."

Chapter Eleven

Fading sunlight forced Anne to wait until the following day to round out Onyx's training. As soon as the lazy orb tipped the horizon, she was on her feet and nabbing seeds from Jacob's stash. "C'mon, Onyx," she said at a hush, slipping the bird from beneath Grace's lifeless arm.

"Let's not wake 'em."

Outside, a stagnant musk hung in the air, and as she breathed it in, Anne felt her lungs grow heavy. She snarled at The Brown, set Onyx on the muddy ground in front of her and told him, "Time to get started." As a refresher, she placed the makeshift talisman near his feet and sprinkled a few seeds on the ground around it. He waddled directly over and began pecking madly. "Good boy, good boy," she applauded, casting a second spray of seeds that fell against the dark ground like tiny stars. "Now for phase two!"

Anne scooped up the talisman and watched silently as Onyx set about vacuuming up the balance of his breakfast. Once he'd finished, she dangled the rock above his head, giggling as he leapt at it.

"C'mon, you kooky bird!" Anne baited him. She lured Onyx towards a group of bare trees that stood like sentinels in front of Jacob's hillside home, and added, "Now watch me." Approaching the shortest of the trees, Anne slowly lifted the necklace and hung it from a low branch. Rustled by the breeze, it began to sway, and Onyx tracked his prize as it shifted back and forth like a hypnotist's charm. "Okay, go get it!"

The raven didn't move. He only watched the talisman briefly and then set his eyes on Anne.

"C'mon, you know what to do," Anne pressed him. She held her hand out and a few seeds trickled from the spaces between her fingers. In a flash, Onyx had retrieved them and abandoned the talisman altogether.

"Darn it!" she snarled, pulling her hand back. "You weren't supposed to get those!"

Undiscouraged, Onyx crept closer to Anne with his eyes fixed on her bulging hand, but she only scowled. "Really? Are we really gonna have to start all over?" She stomped towards the branch where the talisman still hung and snatched it. "Looky, looky. Remember this?" she mocked, dangling it over his head.

Onyx squawked and did a little jig before biting at the air.

"Okay, now we're cookin'." Anne lowered the talisman again and delighted as Onyx pecked at it. She scattered seed, like a halo around him, and continued, "Now, let's try this again," before once again looping the necklace over the lowest branch on the tree. This time, Onyx lifted from the ground and flew directly to it.

"Perfect! Way to go, Onyx!" Anne parted her fingers, offering the entire heap of seed. As he gorged himself, she decided: "A few more rounds like that, and we should be good to go."

Anne's smile swelled along with the raven's belly, until a thud of approaching feet disrupted their celebration. Her eyes flitted towards the cave, but no one appeared there.

"Grace? Jacob?" Anne called, meeting only silence in reply. She panned the small grove in which she stood, completing two full revolutions before a Faerie leapt from behind a tree to her immediate left. It was atop her in a flash, its blank eyes inches from hers. Despite the delicacy of its hands, they felt like iron vices pinning her on the spot. As it examined Anne, the shriveled knot where its mouth ought to have been puckered and pulsed as though about to give birth. In the foreground, Onyx screeched and pecked at the creature, who paid him little mind.

"Grace! Jacob!" Anne shrieked. She flailed and fought but the Faerie maintained his hold and his blank expression. Only a slight tilt of his head, like that of a confused animal, belied his intrigue as her voice curdled the air. Finally, he cupped his right hand over her lips, muffling her cries. His hand was so icy cold that it burned. He lowered his pale face to hers until their noses nearly touched and then drew his eyelids back, exposing eyes like dull marbles. Horror swelled in Anne's gut, as she felt them burrowing inside her. The pain was excruciating. Her vision steadily blackened until only the creature's knot of a mouth, throbbing faster than ever, was visible. In her stupor, the thunk of his body landing on the ground beside her was barely audible.

"Oh, my goodness, are you alright?" Grace breathlessly inquired. Though she stood within inches, her voice sounded far away. A sliver of her harrowed face came into view as the clouds slowly cleared from Anne's eyes.

"Can you move? Can you get up?" Grace glanced sideways at the lifeless creature, and added, "We need to go before it wakes up!"

Grace gave Anne's shoulder a hard shake and tingles crept up her neck like the footsteps of a spider.

"Aye! We can't hang about!" Jacob warned as he appeared at his sister's side. He stooped to retrieve two plum-sized rocks near the body of the unconscious creature who had attacked Anne, exposing a slingshot dangling from his right hand. "She's a sure shot," he added, as Anne stared at it.

Anne nodded approvingly, accepted Grace's extended hand, and pulled herself into a sitting position. Her head reeled and as she drew to her feet, she had to suppress the urge to vomit.

On the return walk to the cave, Anne's legs rattled as though atrophied, and it was only with great effort that Grace managed to steady her enough to get them both over the threshold.

Inside, Jacob immediately barricaded the open doorway with his body while glancing nervously around the room. "Got to move! We've got to move," he railed, breaking from the exit to gather items from around the digout.

"What do you mean? We're in now. We're—we're safe," Grace sputtered between groans. Anne slid from her grip like a limp slug and collapsed onto the girls' sleeping pad.

"We're 'bout as far from safe as we can be," Jacob warned, before depositing his bag of seed and the makeshift talisman into a woven sack. He moved around the cavern quick as a jackrabbit, digging up his various hidey-holes and emptying their contents into his pack. "You think that's it? You think we bested that beast and that'll be that?" he ranted, "Oh no, that's just the start. That critter is gonna wake up, and he's gonna go for reinforcements."

Jacob nodded towards the doorway and then at the girls. "Come sunset there'll be a swarm of 'em out there!"

Anne felt Grace's hand tense on her shoulder. She glanced towards the exit, where the boulder Jacob had used to disguise it was sitting just right of the doorway. Its shadow created a crescent moon on the earth floor and Anne fixed her eyes on it, quaking, until Jacob's footsteps sliced it in two. He walked to the room's center and turned in circle, scanning the digout. "Best we head to The Black now—head towards the talisman. There'll be no comin' back here, not for ages."

Anne lifted her head with a groan of effort. "I…I'm not sure I can make it," she admitted in a voice that sounded not like her own.

Jacob eyeballed her for a moment and then withdrew a vial from his satchel. "Here, sip on this," he directed, walking towards her. He placed the vial in her outstretched hand and assured, "Before ya even ask, it ain't no drug. It won't put ya to sleep. It'll do quite the opposite, matter of fact."

Anne glowered at him briefly and then raised the vial to her hips. As its contents trickled down her throat, she imagined herself growing magically smaller or even so big that she could carry Grace and Jacob all the way to The Black atop her shoulders. Following a final gulp, she lowered the vial and a dirt-like aftertaste kicked up and flooded her mouth. She choked, and her eyes began to water uncontrollably.

"That'd be the worm puree," Jacob said with a snigger.

He turned and hobbled towards the exit, trailing chuckles behind him. On the threshold, he paused and promised, "Be right back," before vanishing with a dusty poof.

Anne and Grace gawked at the empty space left in his wake for several minutes, finally jerking when he reappeared. He was huffing, but still grinning. "He's gone. Probably not long ago, but he's left," Jacob explained. As he turned back around to face the open passage, he added, "Fast as they go, he's probably halfway back home now, craftin' his tattle."

Grace gulped, but said nothing. Her eyes stayed fixed on the hole leading outside. Beside her, Anne stood and was pleased to find firm legs beneath her. "Well, I'll be…" Anne trailed, bending and bouncing. "That nasty stuff really does work!"

"Told ya," Jacob winked.

Grace's focus broke from the exit but her expression remained troubled. "You sure you're all right, Anne?" she asked, studying her friend. "I mean that thing, whatever it did to you. Well, it just seemed…I don't know, like it was draining the life from you."

"I'm sure. I'm okay. See!" Anne galloped across the room and then made a dramatic leap across the crescent shadow, where it still lay like a welcome mat inside the doorway. "And, besides, you guys saved me," she added. She regarded Jacob softly and then turned to Grace with the same warmness. "Thank you."

Jacob's face dipped to the ground beside him, where Onyx stood, looking expectantly upwards. "Real hero is this fella here," Jacob praised, admiring the raven. "Had he not let us know you were being changed, it might well have happened."

"Changed?" Anne felt suddenly weak again.

"Aye. That beast was trying to switch bodies with you. 'Bout managed it, too," Jacob went on. He took up his cane and approached the exit. Straddling the threshold, he paused and panned the digout with wistful eyes. A single tear traced his cheek, and Anne realized he was saying goodbye to his home. He wiped it away and then melted into The Brown.

The girls followed quickly behind and found Jacob standing just a few feet from the cave, scanning the perimeter. He announced that they were "headed to The Grey," and then took off at a brisk pace.

"Wait? What? I thought we had to go get the talisman from The Black," Anne sputtered. She found her belligerence was returning along with her strength.

"Aye," Jacob answered back, not looking at her. "But The Grey is the quickest way there."

Grace loped alongside her brother. "I'm confused," she admitted beneath a dumb look.

"I told ya, Grey's the corridor," Jacob said with a certain snarl. The annoyance in his voice was palpable.

Anne stopped and pinned her hands to her hips. "Yeah, but we traveled from The Brown to The Black and back again before, without even stepping foot in The Grey!" Her lips had worked into a curl.

Jacob came to a standstill and mirrored her look of disgust. "Land's sakes, must I explain everything to ya? Look—The Grey is a faster way to travel. It's lighter, and it, well, it'll get ya farther. It's kinda like a shortcut between the forests. You walk a day in the Grey, and you'll find yourself legions further up in The Black than if you just walked all that while in the dark." His eyes lowered as he confessed, "I'm not full sure how it works," but then lifted again as he told her, "That talisman, it's a ways up in The Black. If we can make up most of that distance in The Grey, all the better."

"Oh, okay," Anne replied with a sniff. Her hands fell to her sides and she muttered, "Sorry," before falling in beside Grace, who'd begun shadowing the fresh footsteps of her brother.

Jacob tore a path through the brush but continually glanced back at the ground they'd traveled, his narrowed eyes scanning the horizon like the return of a typewriter. After the sixth or seventh peek over his shoulder, he decided, "We'd better find a tunnel when we can. I don't like this—being out in the open like this—especially with a horde of Faeries headed our way."

Jacob's cane pushed pinholes in the soggy ground and the girls followed them towards a grove of twisted trees several leagues in the distance. "It's a bit outta the way and likely overgrown," Jacob admitted. He lifted his head and watched silently as Onyx's shadow moved towards the grove, true as an arrow, before whispering, "But it's safer."

Up ahead, a gathering of bare alder trees stood like a mass of porcupine quills. With no leaves to shelter the grove's floor from the sun, a nest of blackberry vines had bloomed there, creating an impenetrable hive. "This looks about as safe as a vivisection," Anne quietly growled as they neared the trees.

Jacob had begun combing the perimeter in search of an opening but paused to glare at her. "Huh?"

"Oh, nothing."

"Here, I think we can get in here," Grace chirped. She was bent down, examining a narrow space between two trees that, while free of brambles, looked barely fit to pass a deck of cards through.

Anne joined her friend and let out a moan before asking, "You call that a way in?"

"It could be," Grace defended herself. She looked to Jacob as he arrived at her side. "What do you think, brother?"

"Ah, that oughta do," Jacob decided. He continued past Anne and approached the opening. Turning to the side, he drew in his gut and then wedged himself into the crevice. Several grunts followed, but as he emerged inside the nest, he announced it was "easy as pie" and motioned for the girls to follow. Grace was next, mimicking the contours of his crooked body before shimmying through the crack.

"Here goes nothin'," Anne decided. She hunched over and drew a deep breath before cramming her body between the trees. The trunk to her rear grated at her back as she squeezed past it, and she felt certain she'd painted it with her own blood. Pausing to wince, she watched as Onyx sailed easily through the opening and into the clearing beyond. After emerging inside the nest, she scoffed, "Yeah, easy as pie alright. Maybe if you're a bird!" and glowered at Jacob and the raven who'd come to rest on his shoulder.

Jacob paid her no mind. The whack, whack, whack of his cane filled the air as he repeatedly struck at the brambles, clearing a path. "I think it's just up here," he called above the clatter. As a clearing emerged, he charged forward, but just as suddenly he dipped from sight. A troubling thump resounded from the blank spot where he'd been, and in the same moment, Onyx shot into the sky like a cannonball.

Grace exclaimed, "Jacob!" and burst towards the spot where her brother had vanished.

Anne hastened behind, arriving alongside her friend just in time to see a fuzzy head peek from between two massive knots of weeds in the earth. "There, right there!" she erupted, pointing at the top of Jacob's head, which lay like a tumbleweed on the forest floor. He turned to face her, revealing flushed cheeks and a sour expression. Anne held back a snicker and watched as he grappled at the ground above him.

"Well, don't ya just stand there!" Jacob demanded, staring daggers at her. "Help me out of this thing!"

Following his extrication from the Faerie trap, Jacob declared, "See, told you. I found it!" and proudly pointed at a tunnel that lay just a few yards away. "Our safe passage!"

"Indeed," Grace bit her lip, then lowered herself to her hands and knees and inched through the narrow opening presented by her brother.

Mimicking her friend, Anne found the passage expanded several leagues in, and she was able to stand. An orange glow flooded the path ahead as Jacob joined her and held out a lit candle. The radiance of the candle's light intensified as it refracted off the shiny twigs that lined the walls of the tunnel. It was a near mirror of the first one that Jacob had led them down.

"Well, then, best be off!" Jacob announced. He charged forward, leaving only darkness in his wake, and so the girls hurried after him, while the sound of Onyx's claws clacking against the woven floor announced their progress. The rhythmic scratch became a pleasant backdrop to their journey, but after a solid hour of listening to it, the sound began to grate on Anne's nerves, and she asked Jacob, "Are these tunnels all over?" if only to hear another noise.

"Aye," Jacob answered back, his eyes fixed forward. "We dug 'em for years. Didn't take long to figure out the Faerie were scared of bein' underground. After we lost a few of our own, well, it just made good sense."

"But I thought the Faerie couldn't take you? I thought you had to give up your free will —to come here of your own accord," Grace interjected. She'd been lagging behind, but hurried her steps to join the conversation.

Jacob glanced back at his sister, the warm candlelight casting streaks across his weathered skin that shone like veins of lava breaking through crusty earth. "True, that's true. But just 'cause they can't change with a body, don't mean they won't try." The shadow of the candle's flames licked at his suddenly grave eyes. "And when that don't work, they'll make a fine time of playin' with ya."

Anne gulped and quickened her steps until she was near her companions. As they continued in the tunnel, she found herself frequently glancing at the emptiness behind her, as it filled with blackness. At one point, she felt certain that a pair of enormous, inky eyes materialized from the dark, and as her gaze lingered, she nearly missed the fork in the path that Jacob had taken. "Hey, wait up," she called, breaking into a jog.

Silently navigating the labyrinth, Jacob did not slow. Two right forks and an incline later, he turned with a grim face and told the girls, "Get ready. We'll break to the surface up ahead."

Anne and Grace linked hands, and Anne forced a smile as Grace gave a squeeze. A perfect oval ring of light beaconed in the dark distance, and as they neared it, Grace's grip tightened.

"It'll be okay," Anne promised.

Grace only nodded, her eyes uncertain.

A round door of braided sticks disguised the exit, and as Jacob swung it open, dim light spilled in. Small steps were notched into the tunnel leading outside, and Grace ascended them so close behind Anne that she nearly skinned her friend's heels. They'd made but two steps on native ground when Jacob swung his arm out and stopped them both in their tracks. "Freeze!" he hissed, panning the forest floor. After several sweeps, his head jerked to the left and then stopped. "Ah hah, just as I figured. Sneaky lil' buggars!"

Jacob pointed at a hollow spot between two banks of bushes and cautioned, "Follow me. Closely!" before approaching it. There, a heap of branches thick with nettles lay on the ground, disguising a hole similar to the one the girls had fallen in when they'd first arrived.

"Those rascals always do this," Jacob snarled. "They always put their traps right near where the tunnels come out." He leaned over and pulled the sticks aside, tossing them into the hole one by one, until there were none. "There, that'll teach 'em."

Turning from the sabotaged trap, Jacob led the girls towards the horizon, where the sun dipped into The Brown, like a cookie into chocolate milk.

"It's getting dark," Anne observed, navigating around a thorn-laden bush in the shadows that resembled a crouching porcupine.

Jacob's head lifted a notch. "Aye. But we're near The Grey. With any luck, sun'll be high there. That one tends to stay out longer."

"How near?" Grace asked between huffs. She'd dodged the porcupine bush and now ran to catch up. As she arrived alongside her brother, he silently held his arm up and pointed at a line of trees not fifty feet ahead. The stand was a dense one, with trunks so congested that no bit of the forest floor appeared between them. Onyx flew towards the grove, turned at an angle and sailed between two trees before vanishing. Only steps behind, Jacob copied the raven's path and disappeared in kind.

"Guess I'm next," Anne said with a shudder. She stepped forward, but felt a tug as Grace hooked her arm. Grace's lower lip was quivering.

"Together?" Grace asked, batting her doe eyes.

"Together."

They breached the wood as Siamese twins. Trees whizzed past the girls like still landscape watched from inside a speeding car. Anne's hair whipped wildly, her slow strides somehow catapulting the two forward as if they moved at one hundred times their true speed. In a breath, they were standing on the edge of The Grey. Anne's hand flew to her throat, which had gone immediately dry, and she realized that Grace was no longer holding it. "Grace?" Turning to face the line of trees behind her, Anne found no trace of her friend. "Grace?"

Dust rose from the road just a short distance ahead, where Jacob had been waiting. He approached with swift steps. "What's going on? Where's Grace?"

"I don't know," Anne admitted, completing a full circle and then returning to her scan of the tree line. "Grace! GRACE!"

"Didn't she come through?"

"Yes, she—" Anne began, but stopped short when she heard the screaming.

Chapter Twelve

"**O**h my God! I see her!" Anne exclaimed.

Grace's flailing arms — and the half-submerged head that accompanied them — appeared as if straight from a horror movie. The chorus of cries that followed added an eerie backdrop, as Grace grappled for solid ground around the bed of sand into which she'd fallen.

A blur of white followed, as Jacob dove to the ground and slid to the edge of the sand pit. Extending his cane across it, he shouted at Anne, "Grab this! Hold it firm on your side!"

Anne felt herself reacting on instinct. She skirted the vat of quicksand, hunkered down near its edge and gripped her side of the cane, holding it flat to the ground. Jacob mirrored her and boomed, "Grab it! Grab it!" until Grace's hands rose like those of a corpse from its grave and gripped down hard on the stick.

"Now pull!" Jacob shouted.

He dug his right heel into the dry earth and banked his weight there. "To the side! Let's pull her to the side!" he added, gripping the cane with both hands and tugging towards the edge of the trap. His face contorted with strain as Anne joined in pulling on the opposite side—Jacob's partner in some life-or-death rowing match. They continued to rail sideways, scooting along the dirt until Grace's neck, chest, and finally legs emerged from the sand. With a mutual grunt of effort they lifted her free of the hole and she collapsed on the firm ground with a sputter. Bits of shiny grey sand peppered her hair, and as she retched, she spat sparkles like dragon's breath.

"Grace! Grace, are you alright?" Anne cried. She crawled to her friend's side and laid a hand on her shoulder.

"I—I think so," Grace choked. A final spray of sand shot from her lips. Onyx had set down just inches from her face and he jumped back as the grains hit his feet. "S—sorry," she coughed, maintaining a gravelly tone.

"Damn, dried up ole' forest!" Jacob spat. As he pulled himself up with the aid of his cane, he glared at the land around him, and added "Good for nothin'," before digressing into a series of inaudible mutters that Anne could only assume were curse words.

Grace sat up slowly and forced a smile as her eyes met with Anne's. "You had me worried," Anne confessed, wiping a clump of sand from her friend's cheek.

"I had me worried." Grace made a half-chuckle and rose to her feet. "Suppose I ought to start looking where I'm going," she said. Her eyes darted back towards the sand pit, where Jacob stood glaring at some point near its middle.

"I 'spect it was no fault of yours," Jacob said, his eyes turning soft as they fell upon Grace. "You even step in this thing?"

Grace's face pinched, and she replied, "Now that I think on it, no…I didn't. We were just dashing through those trees, and then when we emerged, I found myself in it." A rain of sand fell to the earth as she fluffed her apron.

"I figured as much," Jacob growled, casting a steely glare about the perimeter and beyond. "Damn nasty sprites, suckin' everything dry. They suck up any bit o' life they can get their mitts on." He spit into the quicksand and gave it one final glare, before approaching the main road, where he set off with a loud huff.

A cloud of dust rose from Jacob's footsteps and engulfed the girls' feet, as they hurried into it, until they appeared to hover like ghosts. Swimming through the cloud, Grace choked back a cough and weighed heavily on Anne's shoulder. Her eyes were heavy, and they fixed on the ground as the group traveled. An expression of worry lay like a roadmap across her face, but as the miles passed, it began to smooth. Grace's dependence became less and less, her steps decreasingly cautious. After nearly an hour of walking, she finally looked up from her feet and into the horizon. "How long have we been walking?" she asked with a faint whine. "It doesn't look like we've gotten anywhere!"

"That's The Grey for you," Jacob said, not turning to face the girls. Even at a distance, his voice seemed strained, dry. "Walk on forever and seem to be getting nowhere, and then all at once, you are."

180

Anne swallowed, cringing at the sensation of sandpaper grazing her windpipe. "What's with those trees up there? The ones with all the blobs in 'em." She studied the withered thicket ahead, which had seemed within footsteps for the past half hour. "I've seen those things before, in The Brown."

Jacob jolted to a stop and then turned around. His cracked lips dipped to a grimace. "Those are the hives," he explained, wearing a grave expression. "Full of pods, they are. Nasty little Fae babies, suckin' everything dry." He gestured to the endless, dead ground around them, adding, "The Faeries, they put 'em here because all the portals, all the life, feeds into The Grey and they need that to grow. But those things, they milk it dry."

"Eww!" Anne gasped, leering at the grove. The eerie grey sun was sliding from the sky, and as it backlit the trees, the hives suddenly became more defined. Anne traced the outlines of small bodies in several of them, and her stomach curdled.

"The sun's beddin' down," Jacob observed as he copied her line of sight. "We best make up some distance before she's gone." With his cane, he pointed at the ground flanking either side of the road, and warned, "Those sand traps come out more after dark. Hungrier, too."

* * *

Travel in The Grey seemed unending. For hours, they continued on the same dusty road, the horizon never changing. The trees, the sky, even the air they breathed seemed to feed from their bodies as they grew weaker. Anne's legs ached, growing heavier with each step she took. She silently prayed for the journey to end, yet as she raised her head and suddenly found the grove of pods within a stone's throw, she lamented doing so.

Jacob came to a standstill and balanced his weight against his cane. "See, I told you," he wheezed.

The infant-shaped outlines Anne had spied from a distance now melted into black blobs and she stared into the trees' branches, questioning her sanity. A low hum grew as they neared the thicket, and without realizing she'd done so, Anne soon found she'd come within a few feet of one of the pods. The noise was hypnotic, and as it swelled, she flooded with the desire to draw nearer. As she inched closer, the pod responded by warming with an orange glow, and Anne imagined how sublime that warmth would feel against her hand. Unaware of her own actions, she began to rise on her toes, straining to touch it. Just finger-lengths away, she felt a jerk on her shoulder and was pulled backwards, seemingly in slow motion. She watched the cloudless grey sky pass overhead as she sailed through the air, and when she finally landed flat-backed on the ground, the wind was forced from her lungs.

Jacob's face appeared overhead like an apparition. His features were fuzzy, though his mouth was worked into a noticeable snarl and moving fast. Surely, he was shouting, but Anne heard only muffled noises.

Grace appeared next, shaking Anne's shoulder and mouthing gibberish to match her brother's. Her face came into focus slowly, along with her words. "Anne! Anne! Are you alright?"

Anne shook her head, certain she heard a rattle in her brain as she did so. A dull ache tickled at her spine and worked up her back. "What? What happened?" Her words seemed delayed, arriving several seconds after she spoke them.

"Ya about got lured in," Jacob told her, his face now clearly in focus. His redefined features were significantly less pleasant than their blurry counterparts were. "Damn pod put a charm on you. Just about sung you to your grave!" He scowled at the thicket where Anne's pod had once again gone dark. "Even those wee babes are crafty."

Grace was silent beside her brother, the curved line of her frowning mouth growing crisper with each passing second. She reached towards Anne and helped her to rise. "Thanks," Anne mumbled, still struggling to find her bearings.

"You are most welcome," Grace sputtered. She sounded even more threadbare than normal. Her arm felt weak as Anne steadied herself there.

Jacob watched the two briefly, glanced towards the heavens, and then at the trees rimming the road. "It's about time we head over. That sun's fixin' to sleep and I 'spect we're about the right spot to cut on over to The Black." His eyes came to rest on Anne again.

"You able?"

Anne was massaging her tailbone, the sting of her fall coming full circle. Somehow, the pain seemed to ground her, and she answered back "Yes," with a voice that she finally recognized.

"I'm not letting go this time," Grace promised. She notched her fingers through Anne's and made a weak smile that dented her temples and accentuated the heavy bags beneath her eyes.

Anne reached out and brushed back Grace's bangs, revealing smudges of dirt across her forehead. "Me, either."

Linked as one, the girls charged into the tree line with eyes wide open. Jacob cautioned them to "Stay close," just before he and Onyx slid between two skinny alder trees and vanished into the beyond.

"I wonder if I'll ever get used to this?" Anne asked, half-teasing, as they copied Jacob's path and were jettisoned through the gates between the forests. Grace's momentarily cheery face fell dark as they emerged in The Black.

"Girls! Girls! Can you hear me?"

Anne stumbled in the darkness with her free arm combing the air. "Yes. We're here."

Grace's voice joined the chorus, calling "Jacob? Jacob?" his name trembling on her lips. She gripped Anne's hand so tightly that the circulation began to fade.

"Stay where you are!" Jacob boomed. His voice was growing

louder as he neared them. "I'll come to you."

Bits of brush rustled as Jacob made his way. Only Grace's increasingly rapid breathing disrupted his progress. "Keep talking. I'll find you," he urged.

"Here! We're here!" Grace called. Her shrill cry was like that of a wounded bird and sliced through the night air, giving Anne a start. "Jacob! Here! We're here!" she repeated again, perhaps even more frantically.

"Alright. Don't fret. I've gotchya," Jacob soothed her, as his hunched outline materialized in the blackness. Within a few feet, Anne could smell him. "Here, take my hand," he said, reaching out to his sister.

Still linked with Grace, Anne felt a tug as the duo set to motion. Jacob mimicked the path of a snake as he led the girls through several twists and turns in the underbrush. They followed blindly, Anne trailing like the tail end of some elaborate Chinese New Year costume.

"The moon's gone to sleep," Jacob explained as they crested a small hill and then inched down the back side. "We'll have to go to ground and wait 'til she wakes up to make our way to the talisman."

"Go to ground?" Grace shrugged her shoulders, their outline like twin camel humps in the faint light.

"Aye. Got to find us a digout."

Primitive as they were, Anne was eager for the solace of a

digout by the time Jacob located one. It was a near doppelganger of the one they'd stayed in near The Brown's talisman, and by that logic, Anne reasoned they were close to its sister stone.

Following a short nap on the digout's twig-lined belly, Anne was awoken by the sensation of tugging on her arm. "Look! Look!" Grace exclaimed, pointing towards the digout's opening, where silver tentacles worked their way across the ground like massive fingers reaching into the cave. Anne held back a gasp as Onyx flew at the earth and began aggressively pecking at them. "The moonlight—he thinks it's worms," Grace said, chuckling. Anne joined in the laughter, quieting only when Jacob roused.

"Ah, she's up," Jacob grumbled, the weight of sleep still heavy on his lips. He lowered from his sleeping ledge with a moan of labor, and then began panning the digout. After a fruitless search for "forgotten vittles" in various hidey holes, he decided they'd "best head out before that lazy moon slides right outta the sky," and ushered the girls outside.

Even with the aid of moonlight, The Black was near impossible to navigate. The air was thick like tar, and when the full moon ducked behind a large tree or shrub, absolute blackness consumed them. The group formed a chain with Jacob at its head and progress was slow. "It wasn't always this way," Jacob told them as they snaked through a field of long, spiny reeds. "Back when they first took us, it was The Olive. It was green — bright green." His tone grew soft as he surveyed the landscape. "It was actually quite beautiful, once."

Anne hopped over a couple of suspicious blobs in her path, breathed in the rank night air and wondered if Jacob was being truthful or had simply gone mad.

"It's hard to believe," Grace admitted, the slosh of her muddy steps nearly overpowering her soft voice.

"Aye. I 'spose it is." Jacob's head dipped, and Onyx slid down a bit on his left shoulder. The old man drew a breath to continue, but instead only sighed and then fell quiet.

They continued on that way for about an hour, silently penetrating the dark with cautious steps. Each time the moon hid from them, Grace's grip would tighten around Anne's hand while they traversed the mire in blindness. When a large crest bubbled from the land ahead and eclipsed the moon entirely, Anne thought the bones in her fingers might shatter.

"Just up here," Jacob said. He shook the hand linked with his sister's, clearly suffering from the same iron grip. "It's just over this crest."

Anne felt herself being tugged forward as they scaled the mound. The thudding of her heart grew louder, rising from her chest and up through her throat until she could feel it pounding in her temples. She obediently continued upward, panting as she fought the loose dirt that trickled from the hill like sand spilling through an hourglass. Beads of sweat dotted her forehead by the time they arrived at the top.

"Oh…my," Grace whispered as she panned the valley below. They'd come so near it that the moon was enormous, and it cast a spotlight before them, as if illuminating the stage of a play. At the center of the beam sat an island near identical to the one they'd spied upon in The Brown. There, several Faeries milled about, their pale bodies igniting the night. A number of boulders lay across the island, and several of the beings were perched upon them, some sitting, some flat-backed and staring at the sky. Immersed in such dark surroundings, their ivory bodies seemed to glow. They were suddenly mystical, alluring. Anne moved forward a few steps from where the rest of the party had stopped. "I don't remember them glowing like that," she purred, drawing even nearer, without realizing she'd done so.

Jacob scampered up behind her and hooked her arm. "Fool girl!" he growled. "You'll get us all seen!" He gave her a good yank, drawing her backwards until the two stood face to face. He gripped her chin and pulled it close to his, drilling hard with his eyes. A low rumble puffed from his lips, while he cocked his head to one side and then the next, bearing down until their eyelashes nearly touched. "Just as I 'spected!" he spat, spraying her cheeks. "Darn pod put a charm on you! Why just look at you…you're mesmerized!"

"Am not!" Anne defended herself, shaking her head. It tingled, as though she'd just woken from a deep sleep. Her limbs were slightly numb, as they had been during her encounter at the Faerie hive back in The Grey. "I…I just hadn't seen them like that before.

All lit up like that." She glanced back at the enclave crawling with Faeries. Now their unearthly hue seemed more unsettling than magical. "Really, I'm fine."

Jacob leveled his eyes at Anne again and then grew still as stone. His gaze pierced like a dagger, and he held it for an extended silence before releasing her. "We'll have to keep an eye on that one," he whispered to his sister beneath the cloak of his flat hand.

Grace nodded, but winked at Anne as her brother turned away.

"Looks like you're up, my friend," Jacob announced. He walked a few steps up the hill and stopped beside Onyx, who was raking at a worm in the dirt. Called to attention, the raven popped up, the unfortunate worm now dangling from his beak, and watched intently as Jacob dug in his satchel and pulled the makeshift talisman from inside.

"I'm not sure he's ready," Anne admitted after stepping forward with an audible gulp. "We didn't exactly get to finish our training."

While Anne spoke, Onyx's beady eyes rolled from her face to Jacob's and then came to rest on the talisman. He stared at the stone for a brief moment and then leapt towards it.

"Looks like he's well ready to me!" Jacob chuckled, his eyes a-twinkle. He drew the pendant up, until Onyx began squawking madly and dancing as if crossing a hotplate.

Grace stifled a giggle. "I think Jacob's right, Anne. He looks as if he's hot to trot!" She flashed a brilliant smile that Anne hadn't seen in ages.

"Yeah, okay. Let's give it a try."

Anne retrieved Jacob's abandoned pack and then returned to her friends. As she withdrew the seed bag from inside, Onyx scampered in her direction with hunger speeding his every step. She scooped up a handful of the kernels and held it out in front of him. "Okay, let me see the talisman."

Jacob said nothing, but held the talisman out while mooning at Anne's handful of seed. As she set about replicating several of Onyx's training exercises, the old man's stomach let out a melancholy growl.

The raven was an eager student with a near eidetic memory, and when motivated by his gluttony, he was ready to lay down life and limb for the talisman in a matter of minutes. "I only see one problem," Anne decided, while shooing at Onyx as he attempted to scale her leg. She held the talisman high, far from the bird's reach, and confessed, "I'm not sure how we get him to want the other one. You know, the real talisman."

Hush fell over the group. Jacob fingered his chin, staring briefly at Onyx and then at the seed bag. Meanwhile, Grace sprouted winkles at the corners of her eyes, and as time stretched on, her lip set to quivering. Anne could see sobs rising up her throat.

Just moments before his sister was set to lapse into a full breakdown, Jacob announced, "I think I've got it!" and scuttled towards the open seed bag, where he scooped up two heaping handfuls. He turned his back for a moment and when his face reappeared, one handful of seed was missing and little honey-colored sprinkles dotted the corners of his mouth. In a garbled voice, he directed the girls, "Follow me," and dipped to a crawl, still cupping the second helping of seed.

The group inched along the lip of the hill until they'd covered roughly half its length. Anne's palms grew heavy with caked mud and her knees turned tender. When Jacob froze, nearly causing her to plant her head in his derrière, she was simultaneously repulsed and relieved to have stopped.

"Here. Here's where we cut down," Jacob directed. He gestured towards a swath of thick groundcover that blanketed the inner side of the hill. Crawling into the tangle of green, with its scratchy leaves and gnarled branches, Anne found that she missed the mud. Still, the foliage served its purpose well, covering their progress and leading them within inches of the precipice that divided the Faerie isle from the mainland.

So near, the once-human guards became more hideous to Anne's eyes. Their pale, still bodies lay atop the rocks, as if dead. Their enormous ink-pool eyes stared into nothing.

Anne moved up side by side with Jacob and pressed her face to his ear. "Now what?" she whispered.

Jacob silently drew a finger to his lips and rattled the seed in his palm, which drew Onyx near. Another rattle, and the bird began bouncing, his eyes sparkling. Jacob steadied him with a firm hand across the back and then popped up out of the brush like a prairie dog while scanning the island. Grace drew close to Anne's ear, and breathed "What's he doing?" just as Jacob's features flashed with delight. He then lowered to a crouch beside the girls and pointed through the brush at a spot near the center of the isle.

"You see it?" he asked at a hush.

After a few moments of combing the beyond, Grace chirped, "I do!" a bit too loudly.

Jacob glared at his sister from under a furrowed brow and then returned to watching the motionless Faeries. Grace's voice was no louder than the squeak of a mouse, as she muttered, "Sorry," and then turned to Anne. "You see it, don't you?"

Anne shrugged and then strained hard at the scene before her, to no avail. She was preparing a reply, when a glint of light arose near the center of the isle and stole her words away. There, refraction from the moonlight caught the edge of an emerald the size of a book of matches and set it aglow. Hung on a copper chain, it lay on a rock beneath a weeping willow tree with bare branches that raked the ground like claws. "Whoa."

"I recognize it," Grace said in a somber tone. Her eyes had gone glassy. "I remember the very last time I saw that thing," she continued, wiping away a tear as it trailed down her right cheek. "Tobias

192

was wearing it at the Spring Bounty ceremony. It was the last thing I saw, before he vanished into the portal."

Just beside her, Jacob inched closer. "Damn devils," he growled. "Use that charm to get themselves free and then make their prisoner carry it right back in."

"If only he'd known what he had," Grace sighed, still fixed on the stone. "If only he hadn't given it back."

"Well, we're about to get it back!" Jacob lifted from his crouch and then inched to the very lip of the chasm. With Onyx trailing close behind him, they dipped low into the underbrush and skimmed the edge of the drop-off, until in clear view of the talisman, with no Faeries in sight.

Jacob rattled the seed again, calling Onyx to attention, and then lifted his fist up high into the air and cranked his arm back, before lofting the handful across the abyss. Hundreds of tiny golden specs sailed through the sky like shooting stars. Given the distance they'd been forced to travel, several of the seeds plummeted into the darkness of the chasm, but a fortunate few made landfall on the island and Onyx immediately took to wing to pursue them. He landed amidst the spray and began devouring it as if it might vanish into thin air.

Anne glanced nervously from each Faerie to the next, studying their emotionless faces as Onyx gorged himself just feet away. All sat still.

"Oh, my; oh, my; oh, my," chanted Grace. She tore off a branch from one of the bushes in front of them and began wringing it, little leaves falling from her hands like petals would from the fingers of a nervous flower girl. Eyes wide, she gaped, as Onyx bounded from one rock to the next, rescuing stray seeds caught in their crevices. When he arrived at the flat rock where the talisman lay, the raven stopped abruptly and then jerked his head. The necklace was swimming in seed, and he stared at it for a while before resuming his feast. When the final golden nugget disappeared down his gullet, Onyx outstretched his wings as if preparing for flight.

"No, no, no," Anne whispered to herself. "No! Get it! Remember, Onyx. C'mon, get it."

The bird bowed his legs, as though preparing to lift off, but paused just before doing so. He craned towards the necklace and gave it a second look, cocking his head one way and then the other. "C'mon, pea brain," Anne rumbled, staring daggers at him through the bushes.

"Look. Look, Anne, he's doing it." Grace dropped her fistful of leaves and pointed at the raven, who'd begun pecking the copper chain of the talisman.

"Oh…yes, yes, yes," Anne purred.

Grace gripped Anne's wrist, excitement radiating from her fingertips. "Anne, look! He's picking it up!"

Onyx pushed off from the rock with the necklace dangling from his beak. The emerald pendant dragged noisily along the stone as he sailed away and immediately all six Faeries sprung to life. The creature nearest their hiding spot scanned the skyline until he located the gem, which seemed to float through the air on its own as Onyx faded into The Black. As he tracked it, the Faerie began to convulse, as if resurrected from death, and then loped after the raven. He was nimble and faster than flight, which placed him within a feather's length of Onyx just as they both crossed the void. Only a howl of wind called from the abyss as the creature plummeted down it, while Onyx sailed safely to the other side.

In an instant, the five remaining Faeries had arrived at the edge of the cliff. They gaped into the darkness on the opposite side, bobbing their heads and twitching their snub-noses. Their spindly arms swung at their sides as they jerked about, scanning the black for any sign of the talisman. As Onyx set down near Anne, a rustle from the underbrush called their attention and ten empty eyes narrowed on the girls' hiding spot. The hairs on the back of Anne's neck stood on end. Silent seconds ticked by like hours as the creatures stared into the brush, all the while swinging their dead limbs with noses a-twitch. The tallest of the group, a lithe Faerie with a long, hollow face, was the first to deviate, lurching to his right and leveling eyes at the guard beside him. The two stared hard at one another for a minute or two and then stalked to the other side of the isle, shoulder to shoulder. There, they vanished into a cluster of boulders, only to reappear moments later, each holding up one end of a long plank. Anne studied them as they rejoined their pack but startled when a crackle behind the girls drew her attention.

"Looks like trouble," Jacob warned as he emerged from the darkness, accompanied by another crackle. "I'd wager they mean to cross the divide."

Anne clutched her chest and pushed down a twitter that swelled there. "Are—are you serious?" she sputtered. She scooped up the talisman from where Onyx had dropped it at her feet and shoved it down deep in her pants pocket. Her hands were shaking.

Jacob only nodded, turned, and began scaling the brush.

Anne glanced sideways at Grace, whose eyes bulged as she made a hard gulp. The girls silently dipped to a crawl in tandem and then scurried after Jacob as fast as their bodies would take them. When they'd crested the ridge, Anne made a harried glance towards the isle where the Faeries had gathered in a semi-circle and were silently examining one another, each of them as still as stone. Watching them, Anne felt a coldness settling in her bones, and she shuddered before turning away. When her focus redirected her to the dark path ahead, she found Jacob's shaggy white head bobbing down the back side of the hill and then quickly evaporating into the night. Now alone in the blackness, Anne imagined the Faeries' toeless feet thundering across the plank bridge and adrenaline surged through her and set her close behind.

They ran madly through The Black, the pounding of their footsteps outmatched only by the pounding of their hearts. Several leagues in, Grace called ahead to Jacob between huffs. "Where… are…we…going?"

"Digout!" Jacob wheezed in reply, his words barely audible amidst the whoop, whoop, whoop noise created by his cane, as it whipped through the wind.

Anne matched strides with the breathless old man, settling in alongside him at a lope. His beard was twisting with the wind, and his eyes bulged wildly as they took her in. Anne pumped her arms hard, and shouted, "But it's hours away!" while glancing back and forth between his crazy profile and the blackness ahead.

"I…think…I…know…one…closer."

"You think?" Anne spat between pants.

Jacob made a hasty glance over his shoulder and his pace slowed. His head was still bobbing with the rhythm of his steps but he shifted so that his left ear was facing the path from which they'd just come. When Anne turned to question him, she found he'd come to a standstill with Grace at his side.

"What are you doing?" Anne shouted without stopping. The increasing distance between them was filling in with darkness and she could barely make out Jacob's bony white finger as it rose to his lips. She froze.

"They're coming," Grace quietly explained as she approached Anne. "He can hear them." She gestured towards the crook of her arm, where Onyx was cradled. "He says we should all go to the digout. He'll lead them away."

"But…we don't know where it is," Anne weakly protested. She felt a lump rise in her throat as she looked into the distance and saw Jacob's white tuft of hair spring to life and then float west.

"He told me where to go," Grace assured her, before notching her fingers through Anne's and marching them into the nothingness.

For a long while, only their shallow breathing filled the night air as they traversed the mire. After cresting two gentle hills and descending into a heavily wooded valley, Grace's steps slowed and she began muttering to herself. "Alright. That was one, two hills. Then the forest. Now the thicket. 'Look for the thicket,' he said."

"Can I help?" Even in the reassuring stillness, Anne kept her eyes pinned on the path behind them.

"Perhaps," Grace answered back. She was peering into the foliage, squinting so hard that Anne could hear her grunting. "Jacob said to look for six big trees, tucked all in a row and backed by a knoll. He said the entrance was there."

Anne rolled her eyes. In The Black it was near impossible to distinguish any landmarks until they were within feet, sometimes inches. She surveyed the fuzzy outlines of large trees in every direction, and moaned. "Yeah, sounds super-easy to find."

"Wait! Up there!" Grace made a hard left, tugging Anne along. "There they are! Just like he said!"

A dozen straight bands rose in front of them, each pointing to the heavens. As they came nearer, wide trunks appeared between them, revealing the six trees of Jacob's prophecy. Grace approached the two innermost pines, released Onyx, and lowered herself to her hands and knees, where a large, flat rock lay. "Here, help me," she instructed.

The slice of slate weighed fifty-plus pounds, but with some effort, the girls freed it and exposed a tire-sized hole and a tunnel beyond. A briny smell wafted from inside that made Anne feel slightly queasy. "Ladies first," she teased, backing away.

Grace curled her lip and crept into the tunnel, with Anne on her heels. "Good gracious, what is that repugnant stench down there? It's getting stronger," she groaned as the passage dipped deeper into the earth. As the pair descended further, the twig-lined walls grew increasingly moist, until mud seeped through small openings in their thatching. Examining it, Anne recalled a Play-Doh spaghetti grinder she'd had as a child and smiled to herself, until a second odious dose of fish soured the image. "This is nasty," she choked. As the main cave appeared ahead, her empty stomach turned and then made a low rumble.

First in, Grace lowered from the tunnel exit into the cavern, took a couple short steps, and then winced as a splash echoed from her feet. "Ah! It's full of water!" she exclaimed before stumbling backwards and nearly flattening Onyx, who was just inches behind her.

The raven let out a squawk of alarm and glared at his mistress, as she regained her footing.

"Sorry," Grace offered, before bracing herself against the wall just beside the mouth of the tunnel. "Now what?"

"Dunno. Wait for Jacob, I guess." Anne dropped in beside Grace and pushed her body tight against the wall, just out of reach of the black pool that lapped at their toes. The girls sat in silence, listening to the scrape of Onyx's claws against the floor as he waddled over and took up guard in front of them. Even in the blackness, Onyx's eyes shined. Anne gazed at him affectionately and listened again to the scrape, scrape, scrape until her mouth fell open. He wasn't moving.

Grace's voice was trembling as she asked, "Anne…what was that?"

Anne drew a finger to her lips and listened silently as the noise grew louder. It emanated from the open mouth of the tunnel and as the scraping grew near, it was joined by two shiny eyes slithering along the belly of the passage like a viper.

Chapter Thirteen

"**O**h, my goodness! Jacob! What happened?" Grace gushed, as she clamored up the passage to retrieve her brother, who was pulling his limp body along it with bloodied hands.

"Damn beasts drove me right into a thorn bed. I heard 'em comin' 'round the bend and it was the only place to go." Even in the near lightless pit, Jacob's eyes burned bright. He was snarling, and his mouth vibrated with a growl as Grace helped to disgorge him from the tunnel. Once freed, he balanced on one leg and then pointed at the weaker one. "Got me a nasty nick in the process," he added with a wince.

"You sure did!" Anne gawked at a six-inch gash trailing down Jacob's outer thigh. The blood clotted around the wound was deep magenta and the skin surrounding it flushed the same shade. "Why does it look like that?"

"Venom," Jacob replied with gravity. "Them thorns are thick with it." He drew a sharp breath that whistled through his only two teeth. "And it's a nasty sort, too."

Grace dropped to a crouch and drew her face within inches of the laceration. Her nose upturned as she got closer. "Can we do anything? Mend it, perhaps?"

Jacob shook his head and backed to the cavern wall, ushered by a cascade of grunts. As he rested his weight there, his cheeks dappled with rosy spots, the flush growing more pronounced by the second. "Only one thing can help," he sputtered between increasingly labored breaths. "Thyne root. Only thing for it."

In an instant, Grace was standing again. "Alright. Where do we get it?" she hurriedly asked.

Jacob didn't reply but instead gasped and drew a hand to his leg, where plum liquid oozed from between his fingers and rolled down his thigh. "What's happening?" Grace choked, recoiling.

His face now the shade of a ripened beet, Jacob slid down the wall and crumpled into a ball. He sputtered a reply, but only the words "poison" and "purple root" made it out before he lapsed into unconsciousness. His hand fell limp at his side, and without the benefit of pressure, the wound began to gush.

"Jacob!" Grace dove to her brother's side, quickly clamping one hand over the cut. With the other, she gripped his shoulder and gave it a rough shake, which returned her brother's senses. "The root, Jacob. Where do I get it?"

Jacob's eyes were half-closed. His lips parted, but only faint whispers leaked out and Graced leaned in close to funnel them into her ear. After a few intense moments, she made a nod and then pivoted to face Anne. "Come here, Anne. Help me."

Anne approached numbly, feeling as though she'd stepped

through the TV screen while watching one of her mother's real-life E.R. shows.

"Here. I need you to keep the pressure," Grace explained. She clamped Anne's wrist and pulled her nearer.

Anne soon found herself on all fours, uncertain of how she got there. She replaced Grace's hand with her own, though it trembled as she did. The pressure coming from inside the gash was intense, and Anne found she had to bank her weight against the leg just to maintain her grip. Thick, lavender liquid pushed through the spaces between her fingers. "You're going alone?" she asked, watching as Grace stood, transforming into an Amazon.

"There's no other choice." Grace was already halfway up the passage, when her reply trickled behind her. Onyx stood very near Jacob, looking after his mistress with the same harrowed eyes that Anne did, but did not follow.

With Grace gone, stillness settled over the cave. Jacob's breathing grew short and raspy, and his coloring more unnatural. Anne gawked as his face swelled: his wrinkled skin drawing so taut that it shined like a plump grape. Beads of sweat, like dots of dew, trailed down either side of his head. He rocked back and forth, a steady stream of gibberish leaking from his lips. "Damn. Damn, filthy thorns," he muttered. "All these years, never got me. All these years." Wisps of his long, white hair suctioned to his sweaty forehead, creating a curtain over his wild eyes. "Failed 'em, I failed 'em," he droned, staring into nothing.

Anne drew her face very near the old man. "No, Jacob, no. You were trying to save us," she assured. "They got you because you were caught off guard. But you did it. You saved us. We're safe."

Jacob's eyeballs rolled back in his head until their whites were exposed. The crimson veins that lined them had begun to weep and muddy his pupils, like blood seeping into snow. He jerked and drew his head back, before wailing, "It burns! It burns!" as bright red droplets leaked from his eyes sockets.

Anne held her breath and looked on in horror as the old man lost consciousness. She whispered "Jacob?" but he did not rouse. "Jacob? Are you alright?" she asked, this time more insistently, but only the lapping of water in the pool at her feet replied.

After straining through the darkness for several moments, Anne located the white of Jacob's moustache. It ruffled with an exhale of breath, and she puffed "Thank God!" while clutching her chest. Swelling with relief, she fell back against the cave's cool wall, where she continued to stare at her patient.

Minutes ticked by and the fine, white whiskers of Jacob's moustache rose and fell in perfect cadence. Somewhere to the rear of the cave, a drip, drip, drip of water complimented the rhythm of his breathing, and Anne felt herself growing weary. Her limbs ached from days of endless activity, and relaxing against the cave's belly felt heavenly. Drained of the will to fight herself, she'd soon drifted off.

* * *

"Anne! Anne! Wake up!" Grace was gripping Anne's shoulders, her hands like iron vises. She shook so violently that Anne lost her hold over Jacob's wound, which immediately began to sputter blood.

Exclaiming, "Oh, my," Grace replaced Anne's hand with her own and then shooed Onyx, who seemed bent on helping.

"Did you find it?" Anne groggily inquired.

"Here." Following a final swat at Onyx, Grace fished a black root from her apron pocket and laid it at Anne's feet. It was thick and deformed, with fine ivory lines ribbing the base.

"That's it?"

"That's it," Grace echoed. She cupped a second hand over top of the first, dug her heels into the twigs, and pushed back as Jacob's wound threatened to burst. "Would you grind it up?"

"With what?"

Grace replied, at first, with only a grunt, as she pushed her body weight against the increasingly volatile wound. "I don't know. Some rocks, perhaps?"

"Um, okay." Anne panned the cave and the lake that swelled in its belly, but saw only black. She drew to a standing position and inched along the wall, studying her sneakers as they skimmed the lip of the water. A few feet in, she encountered a small stone, and around the back half of the cave, a second. After returning to Grace's side, she plucked the curious root from the ground, sandwiched it between them, and dragged the rocks back and forth.

"We just need a little. It's powerful stuff," Grace explained, her face growing flush with effort. "We just have to dab it on the wound."

Anne parted the rocks and held them up, revealing a grainy cream mash.

"That should do," Grace said. She wiped up a glob of the paste, drew her hands from Jacob's puncture and slathered paste on the top of it.

Both girls stood back and fixed on the trail of cream that illuminated their surroundings. "You think it worked?" Anne asked, narrowing her eyes. The white line appeared unbroken.

Grace dipped her head and examined her handiwork. "I believe it did," she decided. Her smile glittered in the dim light, and Anne returned it, along with a sigh. Grace added a sigh of her own and then collapsed against the inner wall alongside Jacob, where she wilted like a winter flower.

Joining her friend, Anne tucked her legs in tight to her chest and let her head slump onto Grace's shoulder. "You did good," Anne whispered, feeling exhausted by the mere effort it took to speak. When Grace made no reply, she readied a second compliment but deep sleep consumed her before it passed her lips.

* * *

They rose with the moon. The cave was cold—colder than before—and its dampness seemed to have leeched into Anne's bones as she slept. She stretched and yawned, feeling filthy, and calculated how many days it had been since she'd bathed. "Oh, you're already awake," she said with a start. Grace was silent, standing over Jacob with her back to Anne.

"How's he doing?"

"See for yourself."

Anne rubbed her eyes and leaned forward. A small warm spot on her body faded as Onyx drew to his feet and waddled away from the place, where he'd been sleeping beside her. She approached Grace, who'd remained frozen since speaking, and peered over her friend's shoulder at Jacob. His color had reverted to its normal pale shade. "Well, at least he doesn't look like a plum anymore," Anne said, adding a small chuckle. She lowered to her knees to examine his leg and found the strip of white paste was still unbroken. "And it looks like that stuff did the trick," she cheerfully continued. "Hey, Jacob. Wake up. Check out the awesome job your little sister did."

Jacob did not stir. The drip, drip, drip of water filled the cave.

"Jacob?" Anne reached towards the old man and laid a hand on his shoulder. It was cold as ice. She shot up in a flash and stumbled backwards, knocking into Grace, who tumbled to the ground. "Oh, my God. Grace… Is he—?"

Grace did not speak, nor did she make any effort to get up. She lay on the carpet of branches with a hollow look in her eyes, just staring at Jacob. After several minutes of silence she finally turned her attention towards Anne and nodded her head slowly, as if it had somehow grown heavier overnight.

"I— Oh, my God. I'm so sorry," Anne sputtered. She'd never seen a dead person before, and much as she wanted to comfort her friend, she couldn't stop staring at Jacob. His mouth hung slightly ajar, and crusty little spots of purple dappled the visible parts of his tongue. Shriveled as he'd been in life, he seemed even more so in death, as though he'd been sucked dry. "I guess it didn't work. I guess it was too late."

Seconds ticked by, with only the dripping of water into the eerie black lake, breaking the silence. Grace's voice sounded not like her own when finally she spoke. "Yes, too late."

"Oh, but it's not your fault!" Anne assured her. She rose and approached her friend with widening eyes. "You did everything you could!" she insisted. She drew Grace's hand up in hers. It felt nearly as cold as Jacob's. "You were amazing."

Grace only nodded, and continued to numbly gape at her brother, without saying a word.

"Here, come with me," Anne urged, giving Grace's arm a tug before adding, "I don't think you should be in here anymore."

With a little effort, Grace drew to her feet, and Anne led her out of the cave with Onyx trailing close behind. Outside, they stood arm in arm in the silvery moonlight, and Anne patted Grace's hand and then drew her in close.

Grace silently gazed at the heavens, and then whispered, "I have no one," before lowering her face towards the ground.

"The heck you don't!" Anne stepped around, until they were face-to-face, and scooped up Grace's other hand. "You've got me!"

For the first time since they'd woken, Grace truly looked at her friend. "I do?" she asked, a glimmer growing in her eyes.

"You do!"

Grace's mouth worked itself into a smile, though it was strangely forced, as though she'd forgotten how. "I've got you," she repeated, exposing two faint dimples. Like a cherub in an oil painting, she beamed, until a crackling noise rose from a patch of brush to their right and all her color washed away.

The girls exchanged harrowed glances as Anne backed towards the tunnel and then began scanning the dark. "You hear that?" she asked at a whisper.

"I did," Grace quietly replied. She tiptoed towards Anne and linked their hands. "I think we should go."

"But— Should we—? What if—?" Anne panned The Black while mentally revisiting the scene waiting inside the digout. Before she'd determined which the lesser evil was, Grace had tugged her into the darkness. They ran for a long while, panting like hunted animals. The path to The Grey felt clear and strong, as though it was drawing them along in its thirst for life.

About an hour into the trek, they fell to a walk, and the absence of their huffs welcomed-in the stillness of the forest. From there, they forged ahead in silence with only snapping twigs and the occasional flap of Onyx's wings peppering the air. A deep rumble from Grace's belly eventually joined the peculiar chorus, prompting Anne to admit, "I'm starving." She clutched her own stomach, which produced a dull ache that she'd grown accustomed to over the past few days. "You wanna see if we can find some food?"

"Excellent idea," Grace decided, breaking from the path and snaking into the brush that ran alongside it. The moon had slipped to a halfway point in the sky, and she followed one of its metallic beams, which shot through the trees like arrows. "Look for the bushes with the star-shaped leaves," she called out as Anne selected another line of light and followed it in the opposite direction. "That's what Jacob told me."

Anne's path led to a shallow gully brimming with green. It was flanked by a bare ridge that invited the moonlight in, and with its aid, she surveyed the foliage below for tiny stars. Spying one or two potentials, Anne waded into the underbrush, but quickly found that it was dense and overgrown. Just a short ways in, she was already up to her waist, a tart scent drifting from below her as she struggled through the vegetation. Her progress slowed, the deeper she got, and when the earth turned swampy near the gully's center, she realized her legs were all but wedged in the sludge.

"Yeah…this isn't gonna happen," Anne muttered, straining to dislodge her right leg. Following a series of grunts and curses that even Jacob would've blushed at, she turned herself around and began slogging out of the mire. When she reached bare ground, she glowered at her knee-high mud boots and then lifted her head, just in time, to spot the Faerie staring at her from behind a large oak tree.

Anne froze. Even her breathing stopped. She stared back at the being who was similarly still. Though the differences were slight, she realized that she recognized this Faerie. It was a foot or so taller than most, with a long, hollow face: the same one she'd seen at the isle from which they'd stolen the talisman. It shifted its head now, scaling her from head to toe with its almond-shaped eyes. Anne's legs were rooted to the ground. She willed them to move, but no motion would come.

"Anne! You find anything?" Grace's call was distant, but near enough. It broke Anne's stupor, and she took off at a sprint. She'd made it only a yard or so before the Faerie leapt from the shadows and into pursuit. It pounced, covering an unnatural distance in one stride, and landed on her back. They struggled until Anne was pinned beneath its lead-like frame, the creature steadying her thrashing head with its cold, bony hands. Anne's fingers dug into the earth, and she yowled, as dirt wedged beneath her nails. The being eyed her and lowered its massive head very near hers. When their faces were about an inch apart, it stopped and hovered, staring. Their eyes locked briefly before a jolt shook Anne's body, and the creature top-pled to the ground beside her. Grace's face appeared just seconds later, sweat beading her brow. "Are you alright?" she asked. She tossed a bat-shaped tree limb beside the Faerie, and extended a hand, pulling Anne to her feet.

"Um, I think so," Anne said, backing away. The cuff of her jeans brushed against the creature's hand, where it lay motionless beside the scene of their struggle, and she startled as if bitten by a bee. "It jumped me."

Grace nodded and nudged the beast with her foot. Its limbs wobbled like over-cooked spaghetti noodles. "We had better move on. I'm not sure how long it'll stay like this."

"Good idea," Anne agreed. She backed away, but kept a sharp eye fixed on the Faerie's body until it was gobbled up by the dark-ness. Moving forward again, she startled as Onyx swooped from the sky and made a rough landing on her shoulder. "And where were you?" she asked, puffing with the strides of her jog. "Great guard raven you are!"

The bird only gripped his claws tighter and silently bobbed along with the ride, his beady eyes trained on a congested group of trees that was emerging ahead.

"That's it! The passage to The Grey!" Grace called from a few yards ahead. She looked back at Anne and flashed a smile while maintaining her run. Following a chuckle, she added, "You two look silly," while watching Onyx, who was bouncing like a jackhammer.

"Oh, yeah?" Anne giggled, her manner suddenly light. A surge of relief swelled in her as she glanced at the approaching tree line. She galloped to catch Grace, and the girls laughed their way well to the gateway between the forests and halfway through it. However, as they emerged in The Grey, Anne felt a familiar drain, and her giggles died away.

The hive that marked their original route lay a football field away, but even at that distance, Anne could sense its lure. "I'm glad we came in a little closer this direction," she admitted, staring at the grove in the distance. A faint glow of orange swelled in one of the trees nearest them, and she wondered if Grace could see it, too. She looked away, and added, "I don't want to have to go by those pod things again."

"Agreed." Grace was already loping in the opposite direction, puffs of dust rising from her footsteps. Onyx took to flight and followed close behind her, his black outline stark against the dull sky. Feeling momentarily light again, Anne dashed after her friends, but found her footsteps growing heavy in an instant. The Grey's ravenous appetite for energy was overpowering and as they continued on through the arid landscape, it milked their every step. Hours turned to days in the unending bleakness, and Anne soon felt madness rapping at the door to her mind. When Grace announced, "I think I see the portal," she worried she'd imagined it.

"Really?" Anne croaked, her throat gone dry. She copied Grace's line of sight and landed upon the faint outline of a crescent, swaddled in moss. "I think you're right. I think that's it!" she decided.

Grace turned around with a bounce of excitement, but abruptly froze as her eyes moved past Anne and into the distance. She leveled her pointer finger at the horizon, saying nothing.

"What?" Anne asked. She craned over her shoulder, and her mouth dropped. The Faerie who'd attacked her in The Black was galloping towards them on all fours, his black eyes fixed squarely upon her.

Chapter Fourteen

"**R**UN!" Grace's apron strings fluttered behind her like kite streamers, as she lit off in the direction of the portal. Anne fell in close behind, and the ribbons licked at her stomach as both girls pumped their arms and legs. The dry air had turned aggressive, and grains of sand bit at their skin as they strained against its swells. Even the ground grew more treacherous, soft spots of earth materializing into sand traps every other step. Anne leapt and dodged and ducked, chancing anxious glances behind her every few seconds. The Faerie continued to advance, moving at a rate much faster than she and Grace, and her head whipped back and forth between the portal and the image of the charging beast, weighing their chances of escape.

"Think we'll make it?" Anne yelled against the wind, her mouth filling with sand.

Grace shot a panic-stricken look over her shoulder. "I hope so!"

Leagues of bare trees whizzed by in Anne's peripheral vision, as though she were speeding past them on an expressway. True to form, despite their progress, the landscape in The Grey remained unchanged, and then all at once, they'd reached their destination.

"There! There! It's just up ahead!" Grace bolted towards a round doorway that was suddenly within steps. Approaching it, Anne felt she'd aged twenty years since she'd seen it last. "Quick! The talisman! We need it to get through!" Grace shrieked.

Anne skidded to a stop beside her friend and fished the necklace from her pants pocket. She made a brief peek at the horizon; the Faerie was still approaching. He somehow seemed further away. "What do we do with it?" she asked, the brass chain dangling from her fist.

Grace studied the talisman with great interest, finally shrugging her shoulders. "Put it on, perhaps?"

Anne drew the chain out and looped it over both their heads, forcing them to rub shoulders. They linked hands and charged towards the portal, both trembling. "Here goes nothing," Anne whispered.

The shroud of moss covering the gate raked at their hair as they passed under it, weaving its tines in deep. Anne quivered. She could feel the moss working down to the base of her scalp, the scratch of its brushy tentacles grating against her skull. She swallowed hard and continued forward alongside Grace — until she felt a jerk at her head. Attempting another step forward, she realized she could not move. "It won't let me go!" she sputtered while wildly twisting to look at the chain of moss that restrained her. She dug her heels into the ground and gave a hard push that freed her head, but found that her right foot was still somehow snagged. "I still can't get through," she continued. "I'm stuck."

Grace, who was now straining at the other end of the taut talisman chain, glanced backwards. "What do you mean?"

"My foot, it won't move!" Anne replied. She dropped her eyes to the ground, where she spied five ivory fingers wrapped around her ankle. Her heart rate doubled. "Oh, my God!" she pealed, "The Faerie! It's got me!" She jerked her leg, dragging the being's sunken face into view. It leered at her, and strained to pull itself closer, but appeared blocked by some invisible barrier.

"Watch out!" Grace swiveled on one foot, drew her leg up and made a hard kick at the creature's head. It winced and recoiled, releasing Anne's ankle. The resulting kickback sent the girls toppling out of the passage and onto earthly soil on the opposite side, with the talisman propelled ten feet ahead of them. Both Anne and Grace were motionless for a moment or two, and then Grace leapt to her feet, and shouted, "I did it! I did it!" while scowling at the portal gateway, which had returned to a solid mass of dirt. She retrieved the talisman and looped it over her neck.

"You did it, huh?" Anne was still lying flat-backed on the ground and sucked in a long, refreshing breath.

"Oh," Grace said, turning flush. "I mean we did it." She smiled.

The sky never looked so blue. Anne regarded a patch of puffy white clouds passing overhead and then took another deep breath. "Oh, man. It feels good to be back." She sat up and glared at the

Mound before confessing, "I wasn't really sure we'd make it back here."

"Nor was I," Grace replied. She was gaping at the forest, surveying the trees while turning in a circle. Her speed doubled and then doubled again, until she was twirling. Her muddied white apron spun around her like a ballerina's skirt.

Watching her friend, Anne grinned, reminded of a "Swan Lake" rendition she'd seen on public broadcast TV last fall.

Revisiting the white bird etched on the title screen, her face immediately dropped. "Oh, my God! Onyx!"

"Huh?" Grace stopped twirling.

"Onyx! I think we forgot Onyx!" Anne panned the surrounding forest, emptiness welling in her stomach. "I don't remember him coming out with us! I think he's still in The Grey!"

"Oh, no!" Grace joined in searching the landscape, both girls calling out for the raven every few seconds. With each echo of his name, Anne's heart sunk a little more. When their voices drew hoarse, the calls died away. Grace collapsed in a pile of dead leaves, and Anne sulked over to join her. They were silent for a time, both staring numbly at the sealed gateway.

When she finally spoke, Anne's voice was barely a whisper. "We can't go back for him, can we?"

Grace shook her head slowly. "Even if not for the Faerie..." she trailed, "...we don't have the incantation to open the doorway."

She looked down at the empty pockets of her apron, and lamented, "I've no idea where the journal's gone," before returning her focus to the Mound, and adding, "Must be somewhere in there," from her snarled lips.

Tears stung Anne's eyes. She fought them back while Grace did the same. As they departed the scene, it was as if they led the procession from a funeral. They walked the forest in silence, with heads hung low. Watching as her feet passed below her, Anne fell into a daze. She might have been back in the Faerie realm, walking an unending road with only hopelessness on the horizon.

* * *

"I found her! I think I found her!" rang an excited voice. Her stupor broken, Anne drew her eyes up and a velveteen road lined with dilapidated Victorian houses greeted her. A gawky boy of perhaps seventeen was racing down the green, pointing at her, and shouting, "Anne! Anne?"

He skidded to a stop in front of the girls, panting. "Are you Anne? Anne Shelton?" His freckled face shone with perspiration.

Anne nodded.

The boy straightened up and drew his mouth into a wide grin. He glanced over his shoulder, and shouted, "I found her!" in the direction of a cluster of people that milled in the distance. His calls set the group to motion, and they approached at a slow, but determined pace, like a pack of zombies. As they grew nearer, Anne picked her

Aunt Claudia's face from the crowd, and her stomach turned. Her Uncle Pat was just a few steps ahead and wearing a scowl that could have boiled ice water. Grace linked their hands and stepped up beside Anne.

"Girl, you're in a good heap of trouble," Pat bellowed once within earshot.

Claudia dodged past her husband and leapt at Anne, scooping her into an asphyxiating hug. "Oh, Annie! Oh, my little niece! You had me so damn worried!" She pulled back, still holding Anne by the shoulders. Her eyes were rimmed in red, and her plump cheeks, streaked with tears. She studied Anne, her soft features hardening. "Where on earth have you been?" she asked, jogging her head to the left and giving Grace a once-over. "And who the heck is this?"

Grace was still hanging onto Anne's hand. She shuffled nearer and cleared her throat. "Sorry ma'am, I'm Grace...Grace Rowden." Uncomfortable silence filled in the space as Claudia surveyed Grace with narrowed eyes. "I—I–," Grace stumbled. "I was lost in the woods. I was lost and Anne found me."

Claudia raised her brows, and replied, "That so?" never releasing her niece's shoulders.

"Yes, ma'am." Grace flashed one of her dazzling smiles and gazed affectionately at Anne. "She saved me. If not for her, I don't think I'd have ever made it out," she said. After returning her attention to Claudia, Grace looked at her square in the eyes, and added,

"You have an amazing niece, ma'am."

Claudia's grip loosened, and she said, "I 'spose I do," before drawing Anne into a second hearty embrace that lasted far too long.

While gagging on her aunt's cheap perfume, Anne regarded the twenty-some townspeople that had filtered in as they spoke. A few familiar faces appeared in the crowd, all with eyes burrowing a hole through Claudia's backside. Among them was Lexie. She stood beside Pat, timidly waving and looking guilty. The boy who'd first approached the girls was standing to her left, surrounded by five middle-aged men, all wearing fluorescent search-and-rescue vests. "Jeez, you really called the cavalry out," Anne said, following a gulp.

"Well, you've been missing three days!" Claudia growled. A sparkle of sass returned to her eyes, but quickly faded, as she continued, "Even had to call your folks and tell 'em."

"My folks?"

"Yeah. They oughta be here tomorrow. Headed back as soon as I called 'em."

Anne's guts rattled as she envisioned her parents scurrying to gather their belongings amidst frequent exchanges of panic. She didn't realize she'd begun quivering, until one of the men in vests approached her with a fuzzy blanket and draped it over her shoulders. He repeated the same action with Grace and grinned at them from beneath a handlebar moustache, before calling to the group that it was time to return through town. They moved as a unit, clustered in packs of twos and threes. Anne watched amazement bloom on several faces, as they gaped at the Victorian relics that passed on either side, while they walked. Heavy clouds had settled over the valley, and the homes seemed to materialize out of the mist like ghost ships, their mast chimneys cutting through the grey. Several of the structures still shined as if newly built, and the girls marveled at the journal's handiwork while whispers cascaded through the group. A barrel-chested man walking alongside Pat, maintained an even tone, telling him "they must be givin' the ole' town a facelift," and Grace and Anne shared a private snicker.

They soon found themselves entering the forest, where the group continued on its narrow path, single file, like a troupe of mountain climbers. As they progressed and the ring came nearer, Grace reached forward and linked her hand with Anne's, giving it a squeeze. Their eyes met, and Grace flashed the talisman, which still hung around her neck. Anne responded with a knowing nod, and then followed her friend's lead and fell to the rear of the pack. "Do you think it'll work?" she whispered. "Do you think you'll be able to leave?"

Grace shrugged. "I sure hope so," she replied, adding a gulp.

The girls watched intently as each in their party stepped over the perfectly round boulders, as though they were simply a line of rocks in the earth. Grace leered at each effortless step, her grip on Anne's hand growing increasingly tighter.

"You can do this," Anne promised. "We can do this." She squeezed Grace back and studied her eyes, which remained as fixed as the stones of the ring. "Hey," Anne whispered, drawing her friend's attention. "Just think of all the other stuff we've done. I mean, we're pretty awesome." She added a wink at the end, at which Grace silently smirked.

Grace's face grew stony as, side by side, the girls approached the ring, the final pair to cross it. As would dancers in a chorus line, they dipped their toes over in perfect sync and stepped down on the opposite side as mirror images. "Yessss!" Anne rejoiced, watching as her friend released a long-held breath.

Grace clutched her chest and closed her eyes, grinning from ear to ear. As she did, the talisman fell squarely into her palm. She gripped it and gave a hard tug. With a snap, the chain split and she drew it out in front of her, examining its limp, dangling links. The longer she stared, the more her face twisted.

Preceded by a growl, Grace returned to the ring of rocks, dropped the pendant on the boulder nearest her, and drew her foot up before ramming it with the heel of her boot. The pendant split in two, and as it did, a clap echoed through the forest beyond. Anne was dumbstruck.

"Why did you do that?"

"I don't want to go back to that place, ever. I don't want anything to do with it," Grace spat, still wearing an angry face.

"Oh…" Anne trailed. She looked on as Grace sighed and turned from the ring with a new lightness to her movement, before deciding, "I think I get it. Time to move on?"

"Time to move on." Grace beamed, scooped up Anne's hand and pulled her forward along the path. Speeding to a skip, the pair soon joined and then overtook the rest of the party. Several people cheered or clapped as the girls passed, smiles spreading through the crowd like wildfire.

Following several back pats and congratulatory words passed among the searchers, everyone returned to their vehicles and left the girls in the care of Pat and Claudia. Two of the vested men, both with badges shining beneath the neon yellow, approached Pat's SUV, just as the family was set to pile in. They pulled him aside and huddled in the glow of his headlights, talking in low voices as the women climbed inside the car.

Grace found herself sandwiched between Lexie and Anne in the back seat, and she leaned close to Anne before whispering, "What do you think they're talking about?"

Pat's eyes darted towards the cab and then back to the vested men.

"Hard to say," Anne puzzled aloud. She and Grace maintained their focus on the conversation as it dragged on for several minutes, with Pat intermittently glancing back at the car. Finally, he shook hands with each of the uniformed men, mouthed a "Thank you," and joined his family. When he settled in the driver's seat, he leaned across the console and whispered something in Claudia's ear. She silently nodded, but kept her eyes pinned forward.

"What's going on, Dad?" Lexie asked. She'd momentarily torn her eyes from her phone and now craned forward as if watching the culmination of a thriller film.

"Nothin'. Don't worry about it."

Lexie leaned forward another few inches. "C'mon, Dad," she whined. "What's up?"

"Just never mind," Pat's eyes were slits as they appeared in the rearview mirror. "Doesn't concern you."

Lexie collapsed backwards and fell hard against the bench seat, causing Anne and Grace to jerk. The girls' motion caught Lexie's attention, like a predator catching sight of two unsuspecting prey animals. She twisted sideways, and her eyes narrowed on Grace. "What are you wearing?" she growled.

"Clothes." Staring forward, Grace was as still as stone.

Lexie drew back, repositioned herself and perched an elbow on the rim of the back seat. "Why do they look like they're, like, a zillion years old?" Her lip curled.

"Well...they're—rather, I—," Still staring ahead, Grace found her left knee began to rattle along with the engine.

Anne leaned across the seat, casting a shadow over Grace's lap.

"Leave her alone, Lexie."

Lexie copied her cousin's pose, placing the two girls nose to nose. "I will, Anne, just as soon as she tells me where she got those retarded clothes!"

"Lexie!" barked Claudia. She'd swiveled around in her seat and was glaring at her daughter. "You're fixin' to lose that phone again!" she warned. Her reddening cheeks were drawn up in little bags that hung across the bridge of her nose.

"Jesus. Fine! Whatever." Lexie faced forward, rolled her eyes and made some choice mutters before redirecting her tantrum to the Facebook friends in her palm.

The cab was quiet for a time, save the rough escalation of gears as Pat sped along the winding road that led them home. Grace studied the landscape as it passed, her eyes growing increasingly larger by the mile. Pat mimicked her in the rear view, clearly fascinated. "So, Grace," he finally peeped, "Where did those clothes come from?" He cleared his throat and briefly cast his eyes at the dashboard, before adding, "The deputy, he was sorta wonderin' that himself. Wondered what happened…where your folks were."

"Oh…yes. Well—" Grace dawdled.

Anne leaned forward, projecting her voice towards the front seat. "She found 'em, Uncle Pat. The clothes. Her clothes were all nasty, and so she found some in one of those houses in the town." Anne caught his eyes in the mirror and held them. "Apparently one

226

of the houses has this secret cellar that no one messed with. It's got all kinds of stuff in it." She made a quiet wince, and added, "Er, I mean...that's what Grace said."

"Mmmmm." Pat's eyes narrowed further. "So what about her folks?"

"Ummmm." Anne sucked her lower lip into her mouth and gnashed her teeth against it. The absence of her response seemed to cause the engine to grind even louder. Seconds ticked by, and as they mounted, she felt her uncle's suspicion growing. "They, um..." she trailed, filling the silence as best she could.

"It's okay, Anne, there's no need to hide it," Grace interjected. She was expressionless as Anne turned to face her. Staring through the windshield, she continued, "Anne just feels sorry for me, sir. Ashamed. You see, my mother passed when I was very young, and my father had a difficult time. He was sick and couldn't work, so we traveled. We rode the rails." She spoke with such certainty that a vision of the pair grew in Anne's mind: Grace's cheeks rouged with coal beneath a newsboy cap, her father's dirty hands pulling her up on a moving train car. "We ended up in that town...Devlin, I believe they call it. We were camping in one of the old houses." She cleared her throat and dipped her tone a few octaves. "That's where I lost him. That's where he finally left this world." Her eyes were glassy in a flash.

"Oh, oh...I'm sorry," Pat sputtered.

Claudia twisted in her seat, reached into the back and cupped her hands over Grace's. "Oh, you poor lil' thing," she soothed between fresh worry lines.

"I…I had nothing to eat," Grace blubbered, real tears tracing her cheeks. "I went to the forest to find food, but I got lost in there." Her head fell, tears spilling into her lap. "It was so awful in there… so cold…so dark." She drew up and then turned her attention to Anne. "But Anne, she saved me," she breathed, her quivering lips settling into a smile.

Anne responded with an awkward grin, not yet committed to her part in this half-baked soap opera.

"Are you kidding me? Is anyone really buying this crock?" Lexie interrupted. She was still clutching her phone, with one eye fixed on the screen.

"Lexie Marie Booth! I have just about had it with you!" Claudia's face flushed again as it contorted into a scowl. Her hot eyes lingered on her daughter for a few seconds, but tempered as they returned to Grace.

"Don't you worry, sweetie. Everything's gonna be alright now." Claudia patted Grace's hands. "Here," she said, drawing back and reaching towards the floorboard in front of her. "We thought you might be hungry when we found you." She smiled, looking at her niece, and passed several sandwiches, wrapped in plastic wrap, and two bottles of water into the back, where they were promptly devoured.

Pat studied the girls' feast in the rear-view mirror with a tempered look of revulsion. "I'll hafta take you two down to the station in the morning," he said. He made a fleeting glance at the roadway and then returned to the mirror. "Deputy Merkel knew you were beat…said you could come home with us for a good night's rest, but he'll need to sort things out with Grace in the morning."

With half-chewed food still bulging in their cheeks, the girls looked at one another without speaking. Panic crept over Grace's features, growing only more pronounced as she choked down her mouthful of sandwich. She nearly jumped out of her seat when Claudia chimed in, "Here we are, home sweet home!" as they eased into the driveway.

Lexie was unbuckling before the truck came to a stop. She vanished through the front door as the engine died, slamming it behind her. Claudia's gaze lingered on the wilted Christmas wreath that still hung on the door, as it lurched back and forth. "Maybe you girls ought to take our room tonight," she decided, turning to face them. "I know you've got to be exhausted, and Lexie's liable to be up groaning all night."

Pat made a small grumble and followed in the footsteps of his daughter, with the remaining three trailing after. Inside the house, repugnant smells of dust and grease greeted Anne, though she now found them oddly comforting.

"It's so warm!" Grace declared, her face bright. She snaked

through the hallway at Anne's heels, gawking at childhood pictures of Lexie that hung on the wall in a perfect chronological line.

"Here, girls!" Claudia's voice beckoned from her bedroom, where she was spreading a flowered sheet over the top of her comforter. "This should do. Just in case you don't feel up to showering," she said with a forced smile, while scanning the girls from head to toe.

Anne dropped her eyes and studied the dirt trailing down her body. "Thanks," she replied.

"Have a good rest. We'll sort everything out in the morning." Still beaming, Claudia puttered out of the room, closing the door behind her as if leaving a nursery of sleeping infants.

Grace and Anne exchanged a wide-eyed glance as her footsteps faded down the hallway. "That oughta be fun," Anne finally said, collapsing on the bed like a fallen tree. Grace mimicked her, trailing illegible mutters that melted to a hum as both girls succumbed to their exhaustion and drifted to dreams.

Chapter Fifteen

Onyx was tucked close to her thigh, as he'd been on their final eve in the Fae realm. The heat from his body swelled, until Anne's leg began to pepper with sweat. "Onyx, why don't you sleep by Grace, as you've always done?" Anne asked, nudging the raven. He looked up at her and blinked, wiping all reflection from his eyes. In an instant, his became the black, soulless eyes of the Faerie at the portal gate.

Onyx parted his beak, looked her square in the face, and exclaimed, "Wake up, Anne! Wake up and see!"

* * *

Anne bolted awake, spots blurring her vision. She sorted through the dimness, recalling their rescue and the four familiar walls of Claudia's bedroom. Sighing, she traced the vines on her aunt's flowered bed sheets to Grace's motionless head where it lay just against her left leg, still radiating the heat she'd felt in her dream. She smiled, looking fondly upon her slumbering friend, until an odd bit of color caught her eye.

Anne dipped her head and drew closer, until a small pocket torn into the waistband of Grace's dress became visible. With her apron pulled to the side, the contents of the pocket were fully revealed—

the top edge of the lost journal, and a section of root the same magenta color as Jacob's infected blood. Anne stared hard at the items, her confusion building.

It appeared that the diary had been intentionally concealed along with a root that seemed a much more likely antidote than the blackened one that Grace had given to her brother. Finally too perplexed to resist, Anne gripped her friend's shoulder and gave a shake. "Grace! Wake up! What is this stuff? What's going on?"

Startled awake, Grace's eyes shot open. They were as black as pitch.

About the Author

Kristine Kibbee is a Pacific Northwest native with a love of language, nature and animals. Kristine's passion for creative writing began in her early youth and led her to the doors of Washington State University, where she earned a degree in Humanities with a focus in Professional Writing. Kristine has since had works published in The Vancougar, The Salal Review and S/Tick Literary Review, and she's a featured columnist for the nationally syndicated magazine Just Frenchies.

Kristine's novella, "The Mischievous Misadventures of Dewey the Daring," is available on Amazon.com, and her middle-grade fantasy novel, "Whole in the Clouds," was released in 2014 by Zharmae Publishing. Kristine's also penned a comedic collection of dog stories, "Frenchie 'Tails,'" which are short, cheeky, ripe with mischief — and forthcoming soon.

Credits

This book is a work of art produced by
Incorgnito Publishing Press.

Taylor Basillio
Managing Editor

Liga Klavina
Artist

Star Foos
Designer

Daria Lacy
Production/Interior Layout

Janice Bini
Chief Reader

Michael Conant
Publisher

Alysa Scanzanno
Marketing Consultant

Cindy Carra
Marketing Consultant

Marci Designs
Social Media/Web Consultants

November 2015
Incorgnito Publishing Pres